EARTHWORKS

Earthworks

POEMS 1960-1970

Sandra Hochman

NEW YORK | THE VIKING PRESS

First published in 1970 by The Viking Press, Inc.
625 Madison Avenue, New York, N.Y. 10022

Published simultaneously in Canada by
The Macmillan Company of Canada Limited

SBN 670-28729-6

Library of Congress catalog card number: 71-119770

Printed in U.S.A. by Vail-Ballou Press, Inc.

"The Couple," "This Afternoon," "The Goldfish Wife," "The
Inheritance," "The Central Market," "Secrets," "The Storm,"
"This Summer I Am Naked in California" (under the title
"This Summer"), and "Waking in Westchester" originally
appeared in *The New Yorker*. "Not Having a Child," "The
Spy," and "Living without Treasures" originally appeared in
Poetry. Certain of these poems first appeared in *Ambit*, *Antioch
Review*, *Atlantic Monthly*, *Bard College Quarterly Review*,
Bennington Review, *Evergreen Review*, *Glamour*, *Harper's
Bazaar*, *Mademoiselle*, *McCall's*, *Nadada*, *The Nation*, *New
American Review*, *Partisan Review*, *Quarterly Review of
Literature*, *The Reporter*, and *Silo*.

Acknowledgment: To Jonathan Cape, Ltd.: From *I Ask For
Silence*, translated by Alastair Reid and included in *Selected
Poems* of Pablo Neruda, edited by Nathaniel Tarn.

For Perry Knowlton, friend of the earth,
and for my daughter, Ariel

I have lived so much that someday
they will have to forget me forcibly,
rubbing me off the blackboard.
My heart was inexhaustible.

Pablo Neruda
"I Ask for Silence"
(*Translation by Alastair Reid*)

CONTENTS

Maps for the Skin

The Vaudeville Marriage

Love Letters from Asia

Maps
for the
Skin

I wake in a cold sweat
Remembering Asia, the days we
Spent together, traveling
All over.

Remember
Our motel in Cambodia
Where there were no cars at all
And only a few French tourists.

Remember crawling
Up the steps on all fours
With you behind me until
We reached the jaws
Of the great stone Buddha.

"We are here!" I said,
Out of breath, frightened
By the smoothness of the stone
Lips. Then I began to
Swallow tears, dust—

That's all in the past. But
Remember this: what we saw
Was an abandoned city. The jungle
Took over immediately.

Nights like this I think
Of New York New York the garbage
And plastic growing in
Fields, broken summer bottles
In pyramids, the garbage winding
Around the apartment houses.

And here I sleep,

On borrowed air, in sheets
That are not ours.

I can feel your breath as you
Sleep. Do you remember the grass,
The sun, the linnets in the dark
And mysterious houses? I remember
That we were climbing in Cambodia
To renew our lives. Hold me!

Beyond us is the highway. And the cars
Never ending in their weekend flight from cities.

To talk about light years is only
To say that time is what goes on inside the head
Since we cannot imagine light years.
But I do imagine them. That is my trouble, dear
Astronaut, madman, ventriloquist, agent,
I wake up and imagine light years and float
Through the vegetable store, the cleaner's, the
Sad warehouses where my things are stored,
Imagining light years. I am a million
Years away from who I am. I am traveling
Slowly.

You never saw my rib cage. I would lie next to you
Breathing and my ribs would hardly be visible but
They would be there, shiny under the moon, the polished
Bones, and I would watch them go up and down but you
Would not see them. You were off somewhere else dreaming
Of what would be, dreaming of alarms or the slow waking
Of the next day. I don't know what you were dreaming
But blatant as horns in the dream were my questions.

I was sleeping next to you. Fluids
Of my body were endless as ferns.
I contained the ocean and the river bed. I slept
Without waking. And when I woke I heard the snow
Outside the window.
What were we doing?

We were sleeping. Our legs touched.
But you never looked at my arms. You never saw my arms. I had
Hidden them skillfully under a long robe during the daytime
And I had used them to carry baskets and books and flowers
In great brick pots. I had been housekeeping and
Then, before sleep, I rubbed the petals on my palms. And
Watched the endless snow fall down. Crystals in the dark and
I wanted to give you the gift of my very cold arms.

I was not I. You were not me.
My love, papoose out of my thighs,
I rock you in huge cradles
Of my knees,
And I hear your first
Cry in darkness.

Now who am I?
Weeping through my hands
All weedy and yellow with
Dandelion nails and drunken fingers,
Blood tumbling through the
Folds of my footsteps
For this: flesh empty
And stomach all gone.

I wake and cannot find
You in myself, my arrow,
My blue eyed Indian, my
New stick, my marrow,

My nude Indian
In your woolen blanket
On the ledge of the world.
My life. My phoenix-feather.

All summer I've been dragging
My marriage around,
Old skin, odd wounds, I think about
The death of someone young,
Rambling through the thin paths of the woods
While summer sheds its leaves
Silently.

Last night I woke
In a peaceful dream
Where I asked for nothing
But to be
United with the garden, with the sea,
With that stranger whom I loved in dreams
But whom I cannot tell about these things.

We were not making love that summer. I heard the dragonflies.
The way they arrive at night
Is sudden. They have moved up
From the lawn, a silent group of
Shadows on the ceiling. They have
Long legs that bend in the
Middle so they seem at once
To be male ballet dancers doing
Warm-up pliés, but they are insects
Who open up their wings
And will not be anything
But mysteriously exactly what
They are. Dragonflies!

They parade out of the pond,
Out of the past, from their own kingdom
With their own lessons to tell and
Their own stories. While
I lie next to my husband looking at them
I am suddenly reminded of how
One kingdom is made to witness another.

For Mary and John Cheever

If a scroll of silk arrives
It may be this letter
Telling you silence
Is closer to sleep than poems.
    (HELP ME)
There's a sound
Inside my dreams
Close to the shape of zero.
In dreams I move in frozen circles
Looking for the homes I cannot find.
    (I AM HOMELESS)
I sleep in France
In an autobus. I wake up at a place
Where thatched cottages appear
And I'm told they are "inns for the soul."
But there's not one place to rent
And nowhere to go.
    (FOLLOW ME)
It is then that the secret of sleep
Resembles the snowflake. It is then
I forge nails out of nothing at all.
I am hammering footprints on the grass.
I am sleeping inside the curves
Of the frozen zero.
    (EVERYWHERE NOISE AWAKENS MY DREAMS)
Do you understand what Manhattan is like?
Phones ring at night. There is dog turd
Everywhere.
Everywhere there is filth, noise,
Disregard of silence. The wire and the sound
Of banging bells
Are all over my nightgown and my shoes.

If I was a huntress of words
It was because I was a huntress of silence,

And just as the Indians went out to trap
Otter, jackal, swollen pelts of beasts,

So I went trapping silence for myself.

At night I listened
To the fumes, the greased machines,
The end of things.

When a wheel broke, it was not the wheel of life,
Buddha's great wheel of birth and endless death,
It was the pierced flat tire of the car
Dying beneath the windows.

Silence was always close to me:
That moment when I move inside the dream
To pierce things.

I gave my life to learning how to live.
Now that I have organized it all, now that
I have finally found out how to keep my clothes
In order, when to wash and when to sew, how
To control my glands and horny moments,
How to raise a family, which friends to get
Rid of and which to be loyal to, who is
Phony and who is true, how to get rid of
Ambition and how to be thrifty, now that I have
Finally learned how to take off the mask
And be nude in my secret silence,
This life is just about over.

I bought white corduroy slacks, which I'm still wearing,
And in that waxed sun afternoon we went sailing, went
On that spinnaker sea—beyond the sagging wharf,
Out of the distant coast—to that far place where no one
Comes—

And we talked about Japan, about shells, about dreaming
As we steered to a world as clean as a girl's drawing. It
Was brighter than blue crayon on that sea, on that sea
Of inspired designs, on that place of endless crystals,
Endless time, endless eels and sea-bugs, grammar
Of the gulled life. Julian, you were in your prime!

Once upon a time I told you, "Take those wooden shoehorns
Out of all your shoes, Julian, you're too neat!" You shot back,
"Mind your own *business,* Miss Beatnik, if you're so free
Why don't you move out of your father's maid's room and live
On your own?" That settled it.

Remembering all your presents, phone calls—
You'd call to go out for a walk—I place you back
In my imagination—When we walk
Through Central Park and watch the end
Of summer kites bob in the sky. "Life is floating from us,"
I hear you say. I am astonished to hear about
Novels, pencils, paintings, pebbles—You know everything—
Honest man, curious, observant, pushing us all
Into the forbidden places of kindness, you are always
Lonely. And true. You know so much we can learn from! But

On this morning, I center on death. And the serenity
Of a cold country without you.

I was in the blushberries,
Grapes and muscadines,
Peaches and ripe nectarines,
Making salads out of cucumbers,
Grafting seedlings and rootstocks,
Planting onions beside lilac
And grafting new life in the stalk.

I was cooking red tomatoes,
Pods of snap beans, winding
Garlic branches in my hands.

I see you weeping in the hospital. Are
Your arms thin as a carrot?
You do not have to tell me about death—
Onions replace the heart, beet blood
Around the mouth, mud
Spooned out of his thighs,
Bowels in the daybed sheets—
Death spreads as quickly as the seed.

I would like to see what it
Looks like. Is it a mirror?
Or a lump of something?
Or a weed? I want to see
It naked and not be afraid.

I sit on a table
Looking at my body,
Waiting for Dr. Fells to come
Back in the room. His air
Conditioner blurs out the
Noise of other people on
West End Avenue living
In their apartments, boxing
With their shadows.

The body a treasure to squander: the
Soldiers in Asia who will
Not fight. "They refuse to
Move, sir," goes through my
Mind.

The air conditioner
Gunning around and around
Is sucking in my list of
Symptoms, taking my
Secret affairs and dumping
Them out the window, distributing
Them on top of people's heads.

His other window faces on
A courtyard. Once in those
Courtyards clothespickers cried
From West End Avenue
To the Drive, singing,

"I cash clothes," and
In those courtyards
Beggars once arrived
As I dropped them pennies
Wrapped in
Dishrags. "I want to be
A minstrel," I confided
To my grandmother. "I want
To sing in courtyards."

Now, high above a courtyard,
I relieve myself of my body
On a doctor's table. I tell
Him my own story.

Burning with Mist

In Memory of Lily Cushing

All that I wanted
When I once wanted everything
Was this: To be
Allowed to name things.

To discover, like Noah,
The name of each animal,
Saying each name
As if I had invented it—

Each word excites me. I enter into
Names.

Find me in the lists of
All things, in the names
Of berries, nuts, holly.
To turn lists into
Songs is holy.

But more than names—I
Have become that force
Inside the lily in the flush of growth,
Entering the garden, bulb,
Blossom, and shoot,
Untangling myself at the root.

Afterwards,
Clean my body as if it were
A room.

Polish my nails
With lemon oil—
Rub my eyes with
Scouring powder. The
Eyes are made of
Marble.

My tears: tap water.
Clean my body, toes
And fingers. Make me
Wholly insensitive
To pine.

I am olive-skinned
And please do not disturb
Me. Maid, make up the
Room. The rabbis have
Gazed fondly upon me.
The doctors have opened and
Closed my doors. The
Simple friends have
Come in and out of my brain
Like sunspots.

Death
Reduces
Me instantly
To this:
A body.
A whore-poet
In an
Old
Quiet
Room.

Opening the doors—
All night I have repeated
My dream-chant, keeping my fingers
On your arm as you sleep—
Taking it away from me—you have
Taken it—taken it—

The spell is taken away.
I recover. My eyes regain power.
What you have taken is this: my juice
Filled with salt, my moisture that
Is strength—my smoke-skin, my
Fire. It is my dream to one day
Be invisible—

In Beauty I have walked
Through lumberyards, through
The impatient landscape of
Houses falling down—childhood
And separation now appear to me
As pure events. Somewhere, out on
The streets of our childhood ball-throwing
And saying what we meant to say—men and
Women are destroying each other.

Sleep with me. Lie down in
The folds of lumber.

In dreams there is nothing left but
My unwillingness to grow up: I see things
I have never seen before. I eat love: a brick-colored
Liquid in a cup without a saucer. A thick
Substance, odd to find in a cup. I drink my
Life at breakfast. Someone is chanting, "No promises . . ."

And I wrap myself up like a
Muslim—a woman is pure eyes. The
Streets are now waking up now that you
Are taking me—

Where? You lead me through a landscape
Of yellow and red maps turned upside down
The way they turn in sleep
When we are lost in voices—voices—
We no longer live in earth
But somewhere else—a climate without
Boundaries—space without maps—An interior
Jungle, place of bestial cats, where you stand
At the door and I ask, "What are you doing?" and
You answer, "Waiting." I see you standing there
In that place of restless furniture
Where you await the future smelling of lice.

You have always been inside me: You are the Expansion of Arabia,
In you Pope Joan passed through Persia, in Babylonia kings feasted
On your brilliant table, your eyes were gentle as the ocean,
You danced with a glass on your head and one day you came out of
The door—looking for me. I was in pain—my body
The same as an empty village closed on a Sunday. Who will give
You your children? Place their head on your pillows?
Who will show you your life just as it is?

I walk out of invisible boundaries in sleep. Singing
With painful descriptions running into chants. I emerge
From a cathedral of lumber, my fingers
Have touched elm trees, birch, barred green cone-trees
With whirling earth as brazen as the sun
In the tree-cone. I hear the breaking of the trees
As they fall down. I see the lumber in the yard and

In the warehouse. Men in black caps ride on small
Trucks, stare at me—"Who is this girl? This stranger?"
They remark—staring at my shoes and up my legs—

While the
Scales of lumber,
The generous pages, the
Teak doors, the
Two hundred doors lie
Piled like
Brown twisted angels
Silently
Placed on their sides
As they dream of
Our lives.

There was a young girl who sat in a sanatorium
Watching the men land on the moon. She had watched
Herself split down the middle with a crack, she
Had heard the shattering, she was being
Treated for shock. All the king's horses and all
The king's men were trying to put her together again.
She saw the rocket lifting in the sky. It was, she
Told me, "Like watching the Empire State Building
Taking off for a day." She also changed the station
And saw young men wearing bathing suits and
Carrying on their heads great gleaming surfboards
On which to ride through a wave. Then, back
Again, Armstrong was saying good-by to the earth
And his wife. "Turn up the TV," a nervous
Woman said. The girl: "A well-known
Group of gynecologists are mending me. Sewing
Me. Asking me to please sit still." At the hospital
Real men, not men in her imagination, were
Landing on the moon. "Make it strange," said Tolstoy,
Writing about the art of fiction. What could
Be stranger? She sat with her mind fixed to the machine
And slowly, one by one, she saw them descend.
"I am sick Orpheus trying to mend," one man said.
She answered, "I am also trying to descend. I am
Beatrice watching history being born. I am
One with the lune."

Give me a mask to hide from your spies, Father,
So I may walk out in my new disguise
Disguised as who I am. But who was I?

They looked at me with such sad, curious eyes,
The elevator boys, and Father's other *friends*,
Reporting on my movements to my Dad
Who liked to say, "My daughter's all I have,"
As he pressed the bell
And rode from floor to floor of his hotel.

I'm there behind the desk, my suitcase packed,
Leaving for boarding school, behind glass walls
Whispering with sophisticated tact.

Frayed Persian carpets woven in my mind,
The lobby filled with fat, myopic men,
Working for the newly formed U.N.
In turbans, all ignore me as I stand
Apart by all those ashtrays heaped with sand
Waiting to be dropped in my new dress
By an elevator into loneliness.

My distant cousin,
I don't think I noticed you. I was
Too busy listening to the grown-up
Conversations. Then you asked
If I would enlist in your imaginary
Army.

I remember you
Asking me to lie down
On the big red sofa in my
Grandmother's living room. I was
Seven and obedient. You
Asked to remove my socks. My
Shoes. My skirt. You tried
To unfasten my small white
Peter Pan collar. "Don't do that,"
I whispered,
"Or I will go tell my mother."

The living
Room.

I understood
Sea shells. The noise of tears. You
Wanted to be a man in that place
Of objets d'art and windows, where everything
In grown-up lives had gone wrong.

You believed in your body. That small
Boy body with a certainty of its own.
You knew, and I knew, we could be set
Free by our arms.

For Arthur Gregor

Sorrow has made of my world a new condition

Imagine living in a useless island where tea is
Good, the wine is from Portugal, and the main
Church has only a front façade like a piece from
A play—scenery—the back of the church is gone.
I remember visiting Macao. The pedicabs were driven
Aimlessly—old men riding bicycles and taking
Tourists to the fan-tan parlors. There—on the ships—
You could hear the long nights of mah-jongg and gambling
Cards. I went there, wondering what it would be like
To never come back. To hide, for example,
In a small factory where girls attached beads to sweaters,
To duck beneath that table of small stones, never to
Come out. Or slip
Into the cracks of an ancient wooden building where once
Portuguese martinets held their parties and their drills. What
Would it be like, to never leave, to suddenly be lost
In the gambling place where baskets were lowered over heads,
Never to be heard of again?

In St. Thomas, dancing
At a ball given
For the Arts Association where men
In strange headdresses dance with me—who am I?
Where women await the giving of the door prize, I dance
With a pharmacist in red velvet pants
And plastic see-through vest. His black skin
Is moving to the beat, while he admits
His greatest accomplishment is a collection of
Mistresses and a wardrobe of fancy shoes. Who am I
Walking in Macao? Who was I in
Chios looking for a place to inconspicuously go to the
Bathroom without being noticed by a monk? Or
Driving down the Keys—the Florida mangroves

On each side of me? What am I doing in Paris
Where I hunt for masks in the Museum of Man? Or in Belgium
Shoved by tourists marching like blown-up animals in the
Macy Parade?

The desire to disappear, the desire to rid myself of my life—
All of this leads me to places, where, for moments,
I lose the stuff of legs and arms and hair and history
That has carried me everywhere before.

"Why have you come here alone?" asks the pear,
Turning around in the sun. "I'm leaving
Everyone," I said, all summer, babbling to
Dragonflies, while frogs instead of swans
Take over the pond. An Italian gardener,
Annunziato, comes on Sundays to pull weeds
Out of the earth while wrinkles grow in
Weeds around his mouth.

I have pulled out of the garden
Ripe squash, dill, and lettuce
As we bury summer in our salads. The
Great white lily casts out its purple
Tongue as if to tell me, "We are here
But we are fragile and we'll soon be gone."

Whatever it is that I know
Is involved in the knowledge of vegetables.

The tomato is ripe. I am ripe also.
My life tied up with vine and stalk.

It is not enough to praise them. I must know them.
I hunger for the way of broccoli—its
Sensual flower.

Pods come out of the earth.
I burst out of myself. The cabbage
Opens in my own
Eye, ear, and spine. The

Harvest!

In that time never forgotten, never dead
In memory, that fifth grade time when
Spring was so lonely that I sit here now, trembling
To remember, the empty days
When classes were forever. I remember Spindy

And the classroom where we sat
Watching the world she put in front of us
While she fed us the world
From chalk, erasers, pencils. Meanwhile

While we were learning to ferret out the names
Of cities lost in the pink and blue and yellow
Colors of South America, the Nazis
Were holding classes in Berlin
During that time when I was very human.

"What made her lose her marbles?"

That's what we were doing:
Fucking
And spewing light love juice. The
Temples of the mind
Were temples in nipples, pagodas
In the chest, in the holes of the vagina,
Holes of the beautiful
Behind, fingers in the ears. We were
Stuffing up the senses.

O Genital-god
Make me real
As I lie
Down
To be born!
To be loved until
My body goes and
I reach the spirit. We love
Only to reach the spirit—the
Corners of the brain, the water
Which is the fluid sign.

I was born
A goddess of water. Water
Has always been my sign. I
Will break mountains to
Become an ocean—lathe of
Spirit and foam. Do not fear
What I tell you.

Taking off your clothes
In California
Is not like getting undressed
In another place. The ripe
Sun says, "No.
You cannot just admire
Me. You must live with
Me. Take me into your
Body. Sleep close to me."

Here there are no
Buttons and buttonholes.
Everything slides down
From the shoulders.
There's no family. No
Memory. And if money

Talks it does not
Talk to me. Here there
Is strength. Anatomy.
The worship of
Green vines of the body.
The stomach churns
Sunflowers, weeds,
And the eyes are clean.

Explain it?
The mild determination
That we have to be
Alone—
To discover our ears
And creases of the arm
As if we were examining
Terrible, strange,
Sting-proof maps of the skin,

If I am ever lost
Look for me in that land
Where the new body begins.
Where the evening
Lasts until midnight
And the mind is flesh.

Look for me
In that place
Of the Palisades
Where the Glass Chapel IS THE WATER WNICh
Mirrors the moon.

Where the sea-houses
Have creaking doors
That are always open
And the sand is there
With thousands and thousands
Of beds.

Where we stare for hours
At the sun, frightened by no one.
Where the light
Breaks open our palms
And our lifelines
Run down to the sea.

Where the ankles
Are soft as birds' nests.
Where the frozen flowers
Bloom.

Where we run out of tears—
Dreaming always of making love.
Making love with the right side

Of the moon. Where we
Run out of signs and sleep
In the deaf ears of skin.

Now, can you tell me
Why there is reason
To weep?

Even the vulture
Is bent on becoming
More than just carnivorous:
His red neck
Is paved from the brilliance
Of the sun.

At night
There's the sound
Of the shell
Beating as strong
As the heart.

Nothing is human.
I become a ripe plum.
I become mango
And seed.
I burst into who I am.

In California
An old man stands, naked,
In front of his mirror
Saying, "I have
Given the poor
Everything and
Now I am truly rich."
He reminds me

Of the lemur
From Madagascar
Who has prospered,
Unmolested,
In his isolated domain. Yes. We are out here drowning—

Arms embrace
The sunlight.

In the cold air
Of this terrible Winter
I say good-by to my Baby
Aunt, youngest of five
Sisters and brothers, now
Made up in her casket,
Waiting her turn to be buried
When the gravedigger strike
Is settled. But I have been
Saying good-by to her
For years—her lovely diction
Slurred in the telephone—
Telling me "How good
Everyone was to me at
Bellevue" and repeating

Alone   *Alone*
To final switchboards
Of the last
Hotels.

✿

I trace the map: here is
A life, here is some scenery
In the country, the city, a
Cascade of furriers, meals, concerts,
Bars, and the great big
Artificial pearls. Here is a visit from
Me with a present, here is a celebration
For her newborn child, two children,
A husband. The country of my childhood
Where I go shadowing my glamorous
Baby Aunt.

✿

"Not every life is a catastrophe, but most
Lives are," I think, uncomfortable on my
Bridge chair, locked in a modest room
Of the West Side's Riverside Chapel. There
Is no window at my Aunt Moll's funeral.

✻

I listen to the iced voice
Of the old stranger
Performing his liturgy for the dead. I
Read the Bible to myself, instead, poems
In my mind, shutting out his sound.

My young Aunt Moll sat looking in the
Mirror of the medicine cabinet, curling
Her eyelashes and allowing me—an eight-
Year-old brat—
To use the eyelash machine and curl
My own. I see Aunt Moll performing the
Ritual of the mask—first pancake make-up
With a sponge—then orange lipstick—rouge
And powder. I was eight. I knew
Something was the matter! I stood on my toes
And tried on jewelry—great purple glass
Rings rimmed by diamond chips. I rubbed
Her Ponge lipstick on my lips.

✻

I forget—try to forget—
My "accidents" when I was too frightened
To sleep alone and she took me into
Her bedroom to sleep in her double bed. Wetting
Her sheets, waiting for her to come home,
I covered the sheets with her towels. Suddenly,
She opens the bedroom door, turns on the light,

Forgives me, tells me about her date,
Turns off all the lights. She's had too much
To drink. Sweet liquor's
On her breath
Inside the wet bed we hug and fall into sleep.

Here
The tall trees of Ohio
Break in my stomach,
Leaves falling, one by
One, in the sweet juice
Of the body. Here
Is my trunk—thick
Legs holding one million
Empty days. Filled up with
Your seed-trap, your
Spirit-trap in this
Flatland.

Sleeping beauty woke and looked at the ceiling. She was lonely
For the man she had been dreaming about.
Lonely for him and what he did not say
Did not matter.

The man she had been dreaming about was a Fire
Executive. He had gone into the fire extinguishing
Business because he was devoted to
Saving lives and putting out fires and at the same
Time he was a businessman and nothing sold better—

There was a fortune in extinguishing.
She had first heard about him from a fairy
Who worked in television. She had been going
Out with him because he was funny and safe and
Didn't try to molest her and took her to
Television shows. She had met the Fire
Executive during a commercial break that was advertising
Home extinguishers. She had seen him—and saw in his
Face—behind the hurt look in his eyes—
A spark of life so fragile
That she loved him immediately. She wanted to

Cry out, "Dear Prince Charming. Although you are now
Unhappy, everything is going to turn out all right. The
Money from extinguishing means nothing to you. I know
That. You would like to be useful. Someday you will wake
Me up. That will be your mission in life. And you
Will burn deep within me. Me within you. And we shall
Be alive without unnecessary talk and palaver."

However, she was still shy. And the prince
Was busy watching over the fire actors.

Years later, however, they did meet. He was

Fire Extinguisher Extraordinaire. Ambassador to
All Burning Countries. And she was just
About to wake up from his kiss.

What the Old Man Left Me

For Flo Kennedy

There was an old man.
He died.
Only painters came to his funeral.
They sat down. Funeral voices:
"He was here yesterday. Now he is gone."
They all had a gargantuan lunch
Talking about painters, colors,
Themselves among the peacocks.
"This is the way the old man would
Want it to be"—Nothing
At all about the almost
Forgotten old man
Except that he was filled
With spirit, filled with health,
Filled with that crazy kind of joy.

He left me, as a gift,
A basket filled with thread. Hundreds
Of spools—now in hiding—
Lost in the closet—what did
I do with that gift?—I cannot sew.
Hundreds of spools, safety pins,
Needles, straight pins,
All in a gift lost in the closet.

I remember a sewing machine
Of my grandmother's—a Singer
Sewing machine—a Singer with
A thousand gleaming needles
With huge eyes—one for heavy
Cloth—one for silk—
She'd put the needle in
The black machine—thread the needle
With a hundred spools of thread

And then all morning long
     tap tap tap

Putting needles through
Silk and calico, linen and rayon too.
Where is that life where
Things out of raw stuff are made?
Little blouses, underpants, hems sewn,
As if a single shawl
Were enough to make the afternoon,
As if life had its own meaning
That she knew as she kept on sewing.

I sit all morning
At this machine
Stitching up my seams. Typing
Wounds and memories
On this odd machine
That stitches up my dreams.
Out of the great ribbon mouth: Cotton
Images, velvet fantasies,
Fear and odd words spout.
I write of insects and spinnerets,
Of spiders, write of the great
Mass of the sea.

1

Ariel, one true
Miracle of my life, my golden
Sparrow, burning in your crib
As the rain falls over the meadow
And the squirrel corn,
While the fragrant hyacinth
Sleeps in its bed in the rich
Mud of the North, while foamflowers
Climb through small arches of rain, and the sun
Brings lilies and dark blue berries
In cluster, leaf on leaf again,
I wonder how I came to give you life.

2

Here, where the twisted stalks
Of deer grass zigzag
Branches from the tree, where
Honeysuckles trumpet, "All joy
Is in the dark vessels of the skin!"
And thorn apples open their leaves,
I marvel to have made you perfect
As a small plant, you, filled
Up with sunlight and
Fragrant as ferns.

3

And before snow
Covers ivy and bluet
Shall I teach you this old
Summer's lesson
About seeds? About miracles
Of growth? Here are the bursting zinnias,
Asters, prongs

Of phlox—shall I wake you?
Take you out of sleep
And roll you in the apple fields?

    4
And through you
I am born as I lie down
In the seedbox of my own beginnings,
Opening the wild part of me,
Once lost once lost
As I was breathing
In the vines of childhood.

Sky Diving

For Evan Barnett

Being here
Is better than you
Can imagine. My own world.
My own sea. Small
House. Purple thumb. Dazzled
Salad head. Green chambers
Of the heart. Tick. Tick. Green
Head. New fingers. No sound
Of telephones. Jackhammers.
And nothing to do but
To be.

People embrace each other and
Don't mind you stripping in their
Garden. But the lawn man is taking
Away my lawn. My house
Is being raised on a large platform.
They are taking my house away
And moving it to another place. The war
Goes on. The streets are now
Getting noisy and filled with razors.

For Elise and Stanley Kunitz

I find
A small town called Gosier where
The people live this way: There are winding
Streets that go up and down hill, tin
Roofs in the sun, and schools
Separated from the street by screens.
Behind the screens children
Are singing about animals. They carry
Notebooks, lined and empty, in their arms.
They wear yellow woven hats,
Starched shirts and dresses. Crayons
Are sold in the General Store. So are rubber
Bands and water colors and other important
Things I cannot live without: feathers,
Mirrors, ribbons.

In Guadalupe I have excellent dreams.
I redesign the buildings of my life. I meet
Again the people I have loved deeply. The
Days in boarding school appear to me
Better than they used to be: I am on the
Hockey team, I hear every record clearly
As I dance during social hour, I relive
Each day of my life, each day as right
As a leaf. I am sensible, passionate,
And I know what to do with my time. But cannot

Stay.

Blood-red flowers have opened up
Fields of sight and power: watch
Their sexual large mouths bruise
When I touch them, their twisted
Stalks are boxer's legs—fast at the roots
And tight muscle green—
See them dance and spar
Within the great ring of a red clay pot.
Ordinary
Geraniums
Are cheerful
While I am weeping
And growling this
Useless summer of
Endless loneliness
And rain. I use
Their bleeding red
Mouths as my targets.
Once,
As a girl, a long
Time ago, I sat
In a boarding school
Study hall, smelling
The great geraniums
On the windows. They
Were the only thing alive
In that poor place of
Pages—Miss Freund bending
Over Britannicas—while
We pretended to study
Geography, hygiene, throwing
Notes to each other
In the shape of airplanes.
She wanted to escape
From that place: be out at the

Sea where she came from,
Where there are aviaries, rocks, animal
Fur; she wanted to be riding
Slender horses dangerous as wolves. I
Pass my secrets, memories, impossible
Needs to geraniums—those
Tight red flowers—amulets to me
Of everything placed
In the strong spirit of the Center.

From my eyes
I draw strength. Energy.
I burst into who I am: blood-filled
Quarry, body of a woman, filled with
Blue veins running wild through my arms,
Pouched stomach filled with
Seed to be a child, knees
Finely covered by the gong-tilt
Of golden hair,
Sensual openings to the imagination,
Exits and entrances to fluids
Of delight. On this dark night
I thank you, God the magician,
For making me not stone but flesh able
To draw my passion
From either a stone or a miracle.

The atrocity
Of the great elephant
In the Milano Zoo: He is
Chained by his leg to the
Floor. His cage is as large
As he is—just a little larger.
He stands there, looking
At adults and children
Pelting him with peanuts and
Garbage, he looks out of his
Tear-shaped eye circled by pink.

I will save you.

His name is Pepsi. He was a gift
From the American Pepsi-Cola Company
To the city of Milano. I wrote
A letter to the company and asked "Do you
Know what agony this elephant suffers? This
Beast which was named after your beverage?"

I received a reply
On heavy stationery from
The head of the company saying
Zoo conditions in Italy can
Not be helped. He said he was
Taking my letter under advisement.
But there was nothing he could do. He
Ended with a paragraph on zoo
Conditions in general.

I received, a month later, a letter
From the Italian head of the company.
He told me the elephant, Pepsi, had

Been blessed by a cardinal when he was
Given to the Milano Zoo.

I imagine the
Miserable elephant in captivity.
At night I lie awake
Plotting our escape.

I think of the history of the elephant:
Hcroic and courageous beasts
Worshiped in India, thought of as
Holy men in Bangkok, treated with love
Throughout Asia. In my childhood
I saw them wrapped in circus dresses
And made to perform—
Displayed
By managers who found them funny. I
Think of the elephant with a chain
On his leg. I think of his life.
His captivity.

Each night
I prepare our departures.

The house is still a long ribbon of
Rooms—green and slightly frayed. The food
Grew on the tables, Florida oranges
Fell apart in skin thick as a hand, floors
Were waxed in darkness and sunlight shone
Only in the bathroom and the front bedrooms.
There! I look out at the Hudson
Sailing me into the sun. My own river—color
Of scum. I see white birds and far away

The never-land of cliffs and Palisades. Here
Tulips blossom in a red brick pot. O I am
Out of my crib. I grow like a great bulb
Too big for where I am put. "Do we live here?"
"Foreign wars," says my mother as she walks
In high slippers down the corridors. "Hitler,"
Says my nurse, guarding her pocket money
For my toys. "They make a lot of noise,"
Say the neighbors, stamping on the floors
During the evenings when my parents scream.

But I never wake up. It isn't a dream.
Turtles are flushed down the toilet and
Goldfish swim in the large glass bowl
Where pebbles are larger than teeth.

Crystal-Growing

For Haroutian Dederian

I hear the sound. It is mostly
The sound of the sea whining and weeping and suddenly
Letting out its great earthless roar.
It is deafening. I cannot get it out
Of my ears, my nostrils, my belly, my long hair.

It is clear as crystals growing
In a jar. It is the sound of dandelions going
To seed and blowing in the wind like huge great
Shadows which must disappear.

Voyage Home

For Aunt Jewel

Beside a lake
Deep in Jerusalem,
A Jew in a skullcap,
A fisherman,
Sits all day upon old stones.
He mends an old net under
An old sun.
(This is a dream, but God, I swear
Your fisherman is everywhere!)
His net is like the lake,
It ripples on
Scales and yellow blisters
Of his palm
As if a man could hold
For one long day
The tangles of the water.
Let us say
His net resembles the Red Sea
Once crossed by Moses, dark, so slippery.
(God, if you take my life, I'll die
Seeing this net, so slippery.)
Now, flying down
Out of the sun,
A bird comes to
The fisherman,
More angel than a bird, this gull
That perches on a rowboat's hull:
An angel gull with a gold beak
And great white wings. He speaks:
"Forget this mending that has no meaning,
Go back, beyond the temples of Jehoshaphat.
Beyond the tombs of David, go beyond

The tombs they call the tombs of Absalom.
Go fish with men, who cannot drown nets
In Jerusalem." The gull
Returns to the sun. The fisherman
Departs from fisherdom.

Dripping winters
Peer from woodwork in this fake Sistine,
Watch my muscles stretch,
My fingers rest upon the looking glass
Gripping suspect figures.
Adam in the mirror. Who am I?
I have not died, but I have seen my soul
Plunge from ceiling to the bedroom wall,
And so, when I say *death,* I mean each time
I've loved, and could not love, each time I've wept
And could not reach for something which leapt
Over *death*

Opening up the looking glass again.

My love after a long journey comes home.
Wrists of time move as they moved before,
Time pounds on the window and pounds again
And what seems like time is only the rain.
Left with our harvest of salad and Greek vermouth
We hide in the kitchen. An ivory snake's tooth
Is in the kitchen stove and cubes of ice;
Dinner is all we have left of Paradise.
Adam and Eve inside of us who died
Are angry shadows on the windowpane.
I see death in the black spots of a radish.

He lay with his head filled with psalms
Wondering how a boy
Could shed all dreams from his mind
And arise to conquer a giant.
The battle was set for dawn.
All the dark night he lay,
Facing the stars and his God
Without a plan. *Visions, am I to die?*
My mind is caught with the tunes
You taught me when I was a child.
They will not let me arm.
How shall I begin
To think of the battle, the way
To fight my enemy?
Only these songs remain
To keep me company.
When the army was all arrayed,
And Goliath stood in that place
Where he knew the battle would be,
David, armed for the moment of death,
Turned all songs to a stone
And overthrew the flesh.

MIAMI BEACH

Waiting downstairs in the waiting room
Of the Hotel Fontainebleau, I felt elated:
Just at five o'clock
Flowers were placed in a marble vase
And orange gladiolas seemed like spears
Placed in that vase for a thousand years.
Then I fled the palace
Watching sunburnt troops march from Gomorrah.

NORMANDY ISLE

At the age of four on this island I played in the sand
To create twin towers. The jellyfish startled my hand,
But a slippery angel came down to sting at my mind.
I saw one angel crying from a cloud
Change to a sparkling gull, change to a god.
Grief was my angel then; grief that could swim
Under the Christ-fish, over the cherubim.
What angel, what vision, what shrimp hangs in this sky,
Love on its mouth, death in its pure white eye?

LAUDERDALE

Far beyond this garden where the lute
Flutters its dumb approval to our love
A pelican taps on a knotted palm tree
And her music follows me tonight:
Pelican, I'm not your child.
       I weep
And hide behind the fences of this reef
Where every scale shines grief.

I have grown tired of the water tap,
The bowing maids, the telephone messages, the crap.
From now on I will praise the water
That flows down me and to me and from me.
Marl, turf, red sod and barbed root, the dust
Are mint and sacrament.
Here is the household of the apple grass
Above the shut eye-caverns of the worm
And I know both these kingdoms of the earth.
I also know the moon. One snowy-owl
Jogs down from Canada, wing over frozen cloud.
One snowy-wolf confronts me with his open jaw
As I devour seed
Of dandelion from Queen Anne's table weed.
Surely the Khan of Tartary once dwelt
Beneath a tent of felt. O tent of felt!

Remember the immaculate King of Thule
Who ran away from his city every night
To embroider a sail in his tower? The winding spool
And the thread were his only delight
As he sang a song to himself of love and the sun.
I have trailed love down
To the end,
And under the sun
I have heard what the ear refused,
What the eye could not see,
What the mind takes down at night like embroidery.
In a sense, I have been by myself
And have sewn up my grief.
And then?
("Descend," says the King)
To the coral reef.

Electra, do not weep. If you had seen
A mule upon the bed sheets of the Queen
You might have been amused. The child is seer
To jests of vision, and the child can bear
Murder, hoofmarks, the awful slaying,
Queen's laughter, the lover braying;
This kingdom of the animals has been
Subject of the stubbornness of sin.
Child, why do you weep? The burro lies
Down in the dung of tragedy to please.

H.M.S. *Beagle*
                    First night out
In grafted sleep I heard the western gales
Calling the *Beagle* back, hooking our scales
To signs, seasons, herbs, and waterfowls,
Firmament of years, cracked bones and fields
Whaled by leeched seed and all creeping things.
The ship's mate woke me with his whistling,
Which means we'll soon pass Chile, pass Peru,
Coil 'round the waters to an island
Where trees yield dappled fruit and streams of geese
March to the shibboleth of fox teeth,
Slaves sell for buttons, though our gleaming stones
Seem unnatural in savage homes.

We have chosen the sea
Because we are lonely
And resemble
All things that go down.
Sucking the sun
In our silver-finned sea-chests,
We leave antennae touching the sky,
We plummet
In the great hives of water.
Che farà Eurydice?

Go, bleed the waves
And find the blue jail of Eurydice.
The sea-blades wind her fingers in the salt.

(There is no bottom chamber to the sea.)
Find on the tips of waves that drifting face.

1

Two worlds stared at each other for some time,
Then, in a flash, collided. It was dark
But luckily it happened near a park.
Two worlds fell on the branches of one tree.

2

The east of distance west of what is near—
O apple that we long to touch and hear
Oil-painted mauve, a foreign mystery
This real unreal still poised upon a tree.

3

But those who are born blind, or have not heard
About the famed macabre clash of words
Still listen with an ear bent toward the moon,
And wonder if it might fall on their mouth.

The sun beats through her window
                beats upon
A closet stuffed with shoelaces and dolls.
The virgin carved in wormwood, a white book,
A box of delicacies, till it finds
A vessel filled with watermelon rind.
Rind is seafaring inside the jar.
The sun batters her window
                beats upon
A calendar once rippled by a shaft
Of sunlight. She turns in her grafted
Dream, still washing the old man
Who calls to her in pain.
The sun shatters her window
                ringing on
Baskets filled with newly lacquered gourds,
Her stuffed embroidered pillow, *Love the Lord,*
And as she sleeps this Wednesday day of rest
The buzzer of the sun keeps
                ringing on
Her books and dolls, until its brittle noise
Becomes the whitened cistern of her toys.

Give up perfection now and learn to call
Old sounds false, and true sounds beautiful.
We are the summit of the hills we see.
Two wings of sunset beat inside our minds
And we become the sunset and the sun.
Also, pine trees, bending in the earth
Like dancers tipped upon a stage,
Become the silent dancers who are part
Of everything we listened for and thought.
We are the summit of the hills we see—
Matrix of that falcon sun and all
Things renewed inside the eye's whirl.

Revelation

For Manina

That afternoon
In the Egyptian zoo
Two swans arrived. Silently
I watched them float.

Feathers of one swan were changed
Into the scales of copperheads.
I saw the slanted eyes of swans
Open into serpent tongues
Until the eyes of swans became
Slanted eyes of poison snakes.

Two swans into white serpents changed.

My toy made in Japan. It was a gift
Made decorative as any crucifix, though slant eyes throb
Inside the varicose form of my God
And all magic reduces to a spring.

O lantern man! Your scientific ring on ring
Is only sun and flowers and bright pink
Tissue paper crisscrossed in green ink;
Yes, I love you well enough to crawl
Out of this bed, release you from the wall,
But I am at the mercy of my jaw.
I sing of pain
Whacking its way out of the Novocain
Just planted in the warm salve of my chin.
I sing of unguents, Anacin,
Sing cotton, blood, and bone
And sing of wounds licked in a quiet home,
Where wisdom teeth are numbed
Away, and dreams
Wring fantastic pleasure from machines,
Where wisdom and imagination coil—
This is the Toy-Man gallowed on my wall.

On this day we said would be
Our wedding day, we meet inside Penn Station
And take a train to visit my relations—
The train is a mad pony I once knew
Could gallop me to China from the zoo.
It jolts to a mad stop.
Beneath a gray boardwalk
Dunes of sand and old crabs that are dying
Become the world. A few salt birds are flying
Through the long stretch of sea air;
They pass our heads and circle in their weir.
Here's the beach where old umbrellas fell,
Where eyes looked from seaweeds, ears from sea shells,
And the long beach knows words I cannot tell—
If I kept you on the train,
Or in that house, or kept you on the sand—
We have been gone too long. As we walk back
My feet fit in the footsteps of your track.

Bad blood, I have my right hand in the sun. I burn
My hair, my arms, my back, my face, my name,
O I have my God-hand at last in the fiery flame.
I enter light! (I have put on
The tennis sneakers of swift martyrdom.)
I run past palaces and pensions,
Past lost hotels, public Italian johns,
Past the limp bodies of the Acheron.
For I had wanted always to attract,
Not the quick pinches of the maniacs,
The selfish hands of flesh-mongers and quacks,
The selfish ones (Always the ego cracks!)
I would go whoring with the zodiac—
And I shall ride beyond
Deodorants, the clean pillows and quilts,
The shared bath towel, the box of cleaning salts
(For this is not the heart of love that feasts
On someone's marriage sheets)
Though flesh has held me with its feather fingers, I am gone.
Now I have my right hand in the sun.

Walking to your home
I sink my snow boots in the winter chaff;
I am too old to know what brings me here
Except for fear. Perhaps except for love.
Shall we stalk the living room and laugh
Or hum a little to the phonograph?
Inside my child home was a polar bear
Embracing me. Within this darkened lair
I dream again and blood has brought me there.
Time for a good night kiss. Let us kiss twice
Before I sail into this night of ice.

Manhattan
Pastures

Hell's a place
Where lover and beloved
Lip to lip face each other's crime. The man across my quilt
Turns quietly. I read of guilt,
I know guilt is a lie.
I dive
Into the water bed of Charon,
Limbo dissolves my breath, Paolo and Francesca spin
Over my bed to comfort me.
When I turn against a night of restless
Sleep, my book and my beloved fall upon
The wind-stained willows of Acheron.

Lower East
Side, Tower of Babel, pushcarts,
Temple of last year's newspapers covering
The world in shelters of odor,
Lost house, uncurled palace of broom—
Hair wrapped in curlers and braids,
It is you he feels in this gallery
Where plates hang sterilized, lobotomized
On fresh burlap walls, where penciled lines
Of human faces suffer under glass. It is you,
Tent of string and wash flapping toward
The east of Russia, the west of Vienna, he fears
Bobbing through the ice alps on a train, half insane
To reach the nowhere.
                    Beautiful dirt streets,
It is you he walked through in the drawing rooms
Of Paris, where delicate quartets
Played songs of no real Solomon. It is you
He was seeking in the coffins of Greek Islands
(Where everyone sought you), but found
Only red tomatoes walking out of a shoe box. In
The swallowed streets of Chios,
It was you he wanted. It was you in the drugged cafés,
In choked hotels, in mosques, in seas, in the yellow
Peeling bedspreads.

Filth streets, bread-spinning springs of our fathers,
We will sleep in you forever.

1

I am locked in the kitchen, let me out.
Burning in the toaster,
Sizzling in the pan,
Choked in the gas range,
Iced in the kitchen glass,
Broken in the bowl,
I jump out of the cup.
Throw dishrags over my anger,
Crumbs over my head, anoint
Me for the marriage bed.
The bride is buttered, eaten when she's charred.
Her tiger falls into a tub of lard.

2

Under a green comforter,
Waiting for love,
The heart of the city breaks
In my pillow, and down
The streets parade the cats
With wedding tails
And great plumed hats.

3

Underneath the city
There is this: paws of a tiger.
For I have seen true dreams
Are white nights lit by black neon lamps.
I have seen the stripes
Of true and untrue dreams:
There are two gates of sleep; one of Horn
For true visions,
The other, shining, of white Ivory,

Through which ghosts
Send false dreams.

The bridegroom by himself is slain. Ivory
To Horn is chained.

4
I saw a kitten with a tiger's head
Chewing up nine lives. Dead
Sperm lice clinging to his catty snout,
He crawled back to the bag that let him out.
"When you find the Tiger, kill him!" they said.
I could not sleep. I walked about
New York and looked for him.
In the daytime on the park's green lip I stood,
Blood in my mouth flowing like a stream of angry water.
Armed, at night, I ferried the East River,
And pounded on his door. The doorman came,
A blue lion tamer shooing off his game.

5
Snow was falling the first day we walked
Along the river's edge. Rocks
Looking toward Welfare Island seemed a gift
Dropped out of a New England sailing ship.
Gulls followed us in the smoke undertow;
And eye for eye and tooth for tooth and eye for eye
My bridegroom slapped against the river's edge. The
Mayor's house was made of gingerbread.
I could not find the straight path out.

6
In Harlem
We climbed the movie steps

That led us to a market place of dance.
We watched a dark brown woman shake in two.
"I am well, I move my arms," she said.
"Never-never dreams wake up the dead."
At the Palladium
Dancing was praising.
Olive ladies
Moved their mattress bodies from the bed
And feather-danced their boys.
Over the wooden dance floor fell
A thousand moving pennies. Catch them all!
Swaying up and down,
No bodies touched, but all bobbed up and down
Jib-shaped and out of water.

I heard the prancing paws of the greased tiger.

7

We crossed Brooklyn Bridge.
In Brooklyn Heights
I heard the sacrament: "You said you meant—
You said you meant—"
Scaled the ice mountains. The
Tiger-eye was strange. I heard claws
Beating in the Stock Exchange.

8

In the animal hospital:
Jaws of frightened animals. I looked at them,
Afraid to see the hairy cats completely shaved.

9

Near the tiger's bed, my eyes could see
Lovers dancing ceremoniously.
Gracefully, along the corridor,

Geese in slippers danced the varnished floor
Lovingly, lovingly.

On the white pallor of varnishing,
Ladybirds and clock-o-clays could sing.
Bees spun music on the chrome
Of a basin's sun-waxed honeycomb
And jaguars pranced. A chittering toad
Sang to the blue eyes of a hog,
Lovingly.

Lovers, when at last from sweet content
You are caught in dreaming argument,
You will drowse in grass
Under the sea where swans are bound at last,
Lovingly, lovingly.

10

I would like back my jungle gifts, as I now
Understand they were given on the basis of being
Deceived. These gifts are:

One white Mexican bird of peace,
One silver and glass treasure box,
A golden ring,
My kaleidoscope,
One Japanese pen,
One Japanese ink grinder,
One Japanese scroll,
One small fan,
One book about the life of Mozart,
One red velvet crying pillow,
One picked-through book of Mallarmé,
One straw angel,
Two geraniums,

Two pink tablecloths,
One white linen napkin,
Two small candleholders with peacocks on them,
Sugar tongs,
A blue holy book for the Holidays.

That is all that is necessary for me to say to you
At the present moment. I hope you enjoy tearing
My white nightgown and my white toothbrush.

11

I woke and sucked my thumb. My room
Had melted into stones.
Bookcases filled with books were filled with stones.
The dresser drawer was saddled with a stone.
The telephone, all numbers, was a stone.
Uneven stones, inviting all contours,
Were varnished on my pillow.
Stones in the mirror. Cinnabar and stone.
You will find that I am
Ready for lapidation. I wept
And heard the bridegroom call my name.

12

Then Angel Lucifer walked the wall
Past the living room and down the halls
Into my bedroom. He rocked
Me to his fables.

I laid me down to sleep and blurred
My eyes upon his cackling bird. We flew
Into the underworld. My arms
Stuck to his bird's crest, fingers curled
Around his wings. And I was borne
Over the gates of Ivory and Horn.

Wreckers
Drilling and breaking rock
As if New York were one great tooth
Rotten but smiling.
Gloria sits in her studio drilling and breaking boxes.
She is not setting foundations; she is making horses
Talk. She is dis-embalming dolls.
In Manhattan everything is being torn from rock.
Our buildings break. Even the ball,
The gong-ball destroying our buildings,
Breaks. Even tools
Built for destruction break.

Outside my window, wreckers
Trapped in constructions: blond
And black men under helmets of steel, caught in earth. . .
Killing earth. The earth is taken somewhere else.
Where does all the earth go?
Wreckers in uniforms of mesh ride
Jackhammers and dust-machines, gripping
Torches of fire. They are precise. Sea shells,
The French horn, animal and vegetable are streamlined.

Drills,
The drills sound in my head. I toss words
Back at them. I throw them down as part
Of a new foundation.
I hang words over glass.

Who will escape
This tyranny of the T square?
Gloria, commissioned by
No one, sets up her broken dolls.

Riding past mirrors and new office buildings,

She tries to construct
A small tower out of ivory and horn.
Dreams are nails. Her daydreams ring
On linoleum. Here, the man
Who dropped the bomb on Hiroshima, and went insane,
Grabs back his bomb again.
She's shrinking the jowl and the paunch of Diamond Jim Brady
To clean lines.
Glass is broken.

1

The Lord is my hospital.
Birth—in silence. Odd that I should fear
Green sheets and pillows everywhere.
An eyeless needle made me drink
Scared rabbit's milk. Unsewn,
I sprang out of the family wound.
Grew and grew.

Once, in my girlhood, a fat man said
(His voice was wiped, his eyes were glass),
"Please inspect the chloroform and
Winding sheets where we are born. Here in the clinic,
Parades a lineup of the dead.
Leather bells and Hershey bars
Are, each day, so regular,
Here in the clinic, here," he said,
"The dumb procession of the mad."

—Odd that I should say,
"Not here!" As if his hospital
Were made of veins, not stones
And earth and common beams.

2

Beastly Babel of sleeping pills—
You, cast-iron men,
Make cathedrals out of hospitals.
Your women have made you will
Open skulls, lost genitals,
Broken spines, coated tongues—
Hell is all pillows.

3

In the clinic:
When I was born, airplanes
Above Manhattan General wrote
"Injury" and "Injured" in the sky.

Kingdom of bassinets and bed, to
The faithless I say, "Be born and die."
                  And I returned,
Scared as a rabbit.

Venice, you are not
The image of Narcissus in the water,
Not a coffeepot boiling
For a delicate rich finger. You are
Glass (not the beads,
Nor the necklace, nor the ashtray,
Nor the ugly cupids playing with
Themselves), but you are glass
Out of the fire, discarded on a beach,
The surplus of all that is not useful.

And in Venice I play with words.
I say, "Venice the Menace," and walk through gardens
Of alabaster weeds. I say, "Venice is Venus," and stroke
Angels who twirl around clocks. I say,
"Gondola," and say, "Canal,"
And shout, "Giudecca."

                    Once there was a Venetian,
Blind. Blind as a blind could be. She woke up
In the afternoon reciting poetry. And walked down the streets,
And fell into a canal, singing, "I am so damn
Blind I can't see God at all."

                    Angel of meridian,
Time out of the past,
Ladyfingers, broken strings,
Unmade kisses in unmade bedrooms, unheld hands in
Unkept closets, unsaid words to unknown lovers, unknown
Movies in unknown dreams.

                    Once,
I dreamt through a window over the Hudson,
I dreamt of the Palisades over the window,
The window on the one hand,
The Paradise on the other. And words

Floating glass from water.

Objects

For Denise Levertov

Snake-dancing down Greenwich Street, I'm aware of my shoes.
Every object stares, stares at itself like an eye
For sale. The Christmas Eye and the Hardware Eye
And the God Eye, all spill
Their pine needles threaded with snow,
Their figs and halavah immodestly covering each other,
Ropes and nails,
Yes, and the Vegetable Eye, lusty as an apple,
And the threaded eye of crosses.
Blinking at them all, I weep for the good eye!
          Objects frighten me.

Were it not for
These reptile shoes
That I follow—
Shoes pulling toward sewer fans,

Were it not for these reptile shoes
Hissing in front of me
Near the river front, breasted with fish,
I would not be dancing down Greenwich Street.
But I've come back
In black leather boots. (I remember seeing
Russian dancers at the Metropolitan
Clicking heels. I said to Arthur,
"For all I know of God
He may be two tiny red leather boots clicking
One against the other.")
I'm walking down Greenwich Street, lifted
Over water-wheel gutters by my toes.
Joy is in this street. As for the sage,
He stands without his shoes.

New York. "Men are like cars." Dolores
Turned on her bar stool precariously
In Dylan's Bar. "When one goes by . . ."
Her finger pointed to the right
Directly parallel to her right shoulder,
As if to signal a dangerous turn.
"Another comes along."

                    STOP

Locate her listener in a
Crash. White-walled wheels are torn.
Fenders smacked. Front lights and taillights
Burn. The motor's on fire
As we signal, "Help us! Let us out!

Help." The white Ford
Consul's gone.

                    CURVE.

Locate the driver. She wakes up
In a grease-papered hotel.
Hôtel de Londres. TURN. Alex
Gland, painter and ski champion (he says),
Once a mechanic in a Swiss garage,
Now a meterman, moves, white, nude, next to her, charges
In chug tones, "Women should not cry." She signals
From her car-wrecked lips and lies: "Look. I'm not
Crying and I never cry. Men are like cars. When
One goes by . . ."
"—Like cars? Like Cadillacs?—"
"Another comes. No, that's not true, Alex.
You are like birds."

We sing for the dead
Employed by *The Learned Society*.
The clerk files *heart* under the envelope
Meant for *eyes,* the bookkeeper enters
Human hair in her column of numbers,
The public relations expert exploits
Brains, the secretary types *souls*
On white slabs of paper as the office
Boy feeds tubes to the copystat
And receives from his machine a collection
Of *teeth.* "Do you know
There's a dentist who claims the history
Of civilization is the history of human teeth
And all we know of ancient man
Comes right out of his jaw?" *H O. H O. H A W.*
H A W. Once I sang for the dead
At *The Learned Society.* I wailed
"Good morning" in the human phone
With a singing voice less human,
As the president,
And his well-known assistant,
Called a meeting and gave grants
To lunatics and lunar assistants.

In my father's brickyard
I saw walls of brick around me. Bricks
Bricks, so bright they were,
One piled upon the other
Like small red suitcases left in the Gare St. Lazare.

I stood in my father's brickyard
And I wondered where I came from, or if
There was something I could ask him,
Something that we would not stumble on.
—Climbed to my father's office.
Covered with white dust, there were files,
And a desk—and there! My father, curious
As I to know why I had come.
Then I asked him, "Tell me about bricks,"
Thinking that he certainly
Had something about bricks to tell me.
"What is there to tell?"—"About bricks,"
I insisted, "about their names."
He looked through
Papers on his desk, all disarranged,
And asked Mr. Bard, his partner, who
Didn't know; and finding nothing to tell,
He said, "Bricks come from clay and water.
They come from water and clay."

Later, when I walked into the yard,
I looked up and saw my father waving at me,
Standing like an old man
Cemented in the strong window.

One moment before flight, the seagulls long
To trade their perfect movement, and
I, in childhood, pitied them.
Salt tears cripple the wind. I walk
This standard island where mechanics rule
Dreams on an empty stencil. How we long
For movement in this landscape.

1

He wishes to be remembered
Not as someone who repeated
Observances. Not as a poet,
But as a husband. And when that failed,
A lover. And when that failed,
A tourist with a glass shield in his eyes
Who, for a nickel, took a cruise and saw
The skyline of Manhattan
Carved from blue cinder.
And when that fails,
He prefers to be remembered as a seal,
Simply a mammal who endured his life.
Captivity. Like one of those brown jokers
In the entrance to the zoo: clowning
A little, showing off, sunning, a flap
Of the arms, a lazy snooze, then dive
From rock to pool.
Having no alternative: happily tamed to do
What the mammal in captivity, to save
His skin, must do.

2

Do not run to the nearest shelter. Awake.
Love is cawing. A particular white crow,
He opens his breast to fly. He dazzles
Us, then preens. Do not run for the nearest shelter.
Awake. For love's a
Black dove all this time. Hairy
And dull, he will hold anything
Between his claws
Preening and devouring our mornings.

3

This should have been our mornings:
Energetic and believable. Sky
Above our city scratched with beasts,
Ground coffee before speaking. Books
On the tables. Cool water and soap,
And little to be eaten. (Fruit sellers
Scurrying in the streets.) Dressing, working,
Answering the doorbell.
Cleaning. Dusting. Dying.
Then rebirth in the market!
Hoyden things! A hookah pipe, mixture
Of melons, artichokes, sausages, fruit
In every form—rectangles and circles—
Honey with a spine of wax. Fish
In a ribbon catch. Dried onions
And peppers dangling on a line. Centuries
Of cheese spilling milk.

I hear you, like a tame seal,
Barking on a xylophone
Your theme song: *Let me
Be free one more morning.*

Crossing the Drive,
The nurse told her future: "When you grow up
You'll be a baboon."

Her parents pretended they were not happy
Piled up like rowboats lying on their sides
And picked themselves up for new boats and correspondents.

And she saw
Many boarding schools. And dreamt of tugboats.
Later still, sun. And a kidnap:
Nothing is as important as a pencil. Write this down.

At that moment
Saved by the boy scouts who happened
To be marching in the hills during
Her kidnap. New correspondences
And college. And a battered man, a quack in a hotel

Room saying, "When I write
I never put all my eggs in one basket." Voyages. Birds
Wore tweed flat hats with tiny beaks.
She stared, that year, at jawfuls of the sun.

1

Suddenly
I am discharged from my job
In a dream of numbers. Coins
Hiss. This is Wall Street: gold
Bricks glitter. There was a salmon
In a pack of bills, remember?
Within the files
Mr. Frank Organ, chief of the department,
Said, "It is the most important section of the Bank
When people need it. When people don't need it,
It is the most forgotten." All written material,
Memoranda, papers, slips, checks, scribbles,
Are kept for at least thirty years.
Mr. Organ supervises over 30,000 boxes
Of records. None of them get away.
"Look here, Mr. Organ, how the sea glitters!"
Bank of Banks. Good-by to your coin shelters.

2

Women, mostly fat,
Mopped the ladies' room,
And underneath the rest room,
Beyond the guards holding guns
Like real cops without robbers,
Men were burning money.
They worked hard, all day, burning money,
Shoveling it into vats.
Upstairs, a man took a photograph
In the photograph cubicle. Painters,
Carpenters, cabinetmakers,
Money counters, women sorting checks,
Women in the Health Department
And in the Foreign Department,
And retirement counselors,

And personnel counselors,
And receptionists
Sat above the flames. Arithmetic
Went on through the bars.

Beginning tomorrow, elevator
Men, carpenters, new employees,
Will have their fingerprints checked.
Everyone will be inspected before leaving
The Bank of Banks.

A farm. A cannon on a hill.
Long ago I sat beneath that cannon
And picked clover. Often, at sunset,
I walked down to the barn, and held my arm
Around a calf, or took the one-eyed pony for a ride.
Later, I walked in the forests of corn.
The stalks were palm boughs, strands of yellow sun.
Evenings, I picked tomato vines.
Earth clung to them, they prickled in my hand.
And our house was always lit. My grandfather
Furnished it from his *Broadway Theatrical Warehouse.*
Everything only seemed to be what it was: cupboards
Didn't open, prop tables had three sides,
Books were cardboard thick, lamps dimmed on,
Statuettes were paper silhouettes—
Papier-mâché, they seemed to have no weight upon the farm.
Even the cannon had come home
From a play about war. It had been in
A smash hit in which Nazis, like
Chippewas, lost. There it stood,
Up on our hill, made out of wood,
Soggy and warping from the summer rain.

Cannon Hill Farm was sold. Black
Out. Nothing works but a kitchen knife.

—36 Rue de Lille

Arms, hooves,
Amputated, floating on
The walls, as they might appear in a dream.

Subletting the gargantuan
Paris apartment of Madame
Foumenille—36 Rue de Lille—
We were visitors in her bedroom. What
Surprised us were murals
Running in a film of white paint:
Naked men and women clustered on her walls
Enjoying each other in a bacchanal.
Caught on the wall, without embarrassment,
Protruding male organs, buttocks,
Exaggerated breasts, dismembered heads
Of—the happy
Greeks—the gods!
By our bed,
A naked man popped out of an oyster shell.
Over the fireplace, great
Horses, open-mouthed, with open-mouthed foam,
Ears flattened to their manes, devoured
Polite virgins. The furniture
Raised unnecessary hurdles
For goddesses. The horse-men
Had them all.
The photographs
On Madame Foumenille's dresser
Stared at the walls. Watching the Greek
Seduction from his faded icon frame, a Russian general
Stuffed his mustache flat against the glass;
Caught in his deva uniform,
He blushed, tipsy and aghast, agonized
By withered gods and goddesses. Our galloping white horses.

I am hungry for the bakeries, not
Their bread. I am hungry for the road
That ran through every country,
And the tree turning color from the south
Up to the north. I am hungry for the salt,
Famished for the shields of odor,
Flags of color, but I will not eat.

Flesh, you are going.
Having given up the taste for meat,
I have given up the taste for fruit.
I have given up the taste for cheese. Salads
And weeds do not tempt me. Thirst is gone.

—but I'll never find him.
I'll open my bed for a secret. And
Hang up my clothes.
Become an old woman in three days.

I turn a song of rooms,
My pages are white ceilings filled with light.
Of all the things inside my room,
The oak working table, and the bed,
The books and records, pictures, of it all
By far the most beautiful
Is the black music stand.

The room drifts back
Into the black iron music stand.

1

A fireman enters. He entertains us
With his water gun, struts around the building,
Warns us not to "use the incinerator."
"What shall we use?"
The fireman enters the flame,
The buildings burn. He waves inside the ruins.

2

I placed inside my hair,
After the flames,
Three peacock feathers, each
With a perfect quill.
I know they will change with the color of morning light
As eyes take on new colors when we cry.
I placed inside my hair
A new eyesight. The peacock walks my forehead as I lie
Alone.

3

Grief enters new cities on
A matchstick.
Grief's in the garage, Grief's in
The windshield; Grief
Is the fireman.

1

"Doctor, voices appear to me in forms
Human and desperate, each in its own body,
Bending, running tiptoe on a screen
As if in bed. *Do you know what I mean?*
Sounds in cushions, silent-movie frames,
Words, naked in Alphabet: alphabet forms:
Y's and *W*'s open-armed,
I's and *B*'s kissing with huge lips—
The camera shifts to *J*'s and *B*'s as black *R*
Clinches white.
                                    Doctor,
I'd like to be a film maker
Shooting naked letters—hidden under
The pillow, through a mesh of swan
And ticking—caught, you know, by the arm:
Close-up. But there is nothing new—
Silence, and leisure—"

2

"In solitude one knows the maxims of the body:
Neon light—over the belly—
The first maxim:
                    If you cannot love
                    Unhook your arms.
Lit by a flashlight:
                        If you cannot love
                        Unhook your head."

3

She sleeps in a bed
Of sweat
Completely vertical
Wondering how things

Will turn out at her funeral. Her
Death is simple and unfortunate.

This was her diary as a virgin:
"Reading the life of Anna Pavlova
Studiously in the tub,
I wonder if love is the same sensation
As the bath water's flowing motion."

—5 Rue d'Alger

Eros and her brother lived
In a house that was not a house,
Slept in a bed
That was not a bed,
Found a maid that was not a maid
But a monster called Agapé.

And they lived this way: Agapé
Wore black skirts, white aprons
Stiff as linoleum, and collected American
Stamps from Eros. Agapé preferred stamps
With white portraits of Abraham Lincoln
Pressed like a cameo against a pink background
And took

Stamps home to her chamber of maids
Where she cared for two children of her
Own. "Look, children!" she would say in Great
French, and they would press the stamps
Against their foreheads and pretend
They were sending themselves to America.

Eros and her brother, who was not
Her brother but her husband, could not

Sleep. Eros awoke and said, "Listen! I hear
A terrible noise in my love-ear. Outside
Our window there's a fallout of
Atoms, airplanes, automobiles,
And clanging ash cans." (Everything deadly
Began with an *A*.) After that,
The cave blew up. Agapé collected her stamps
And ran home. The bed rocked to splinters

And out of the splinters rolled Eros
And her brother. Rolled into the street. Out
Of the street into the earth. "Merde!"
Screamed Agapé. "I feel the loneliness of
Their dreams in mine."

In the end
There will be nothing but a hairbrush.
I shall find the bristles to be soft. Brush
My hair, and with my hair my mind
And unknown cavities of water.
I shall brush and tease. Until pools of memory
Are like all strands of hair: soft,
So clean, or singed.

Where Puerto Ricans
Squash seeds with ripe feet
And baby Hebrews dance to school,
Their curls
Dangling from manly suède hats,
I heard a voice
Singing clearly to me: "Don't
Speak with men but with angels."

I dreamt of my dead grandfather
Who once lived on St. Mark's Place.
For a nickel he would minstrel
In the parks, or jostle hot dogs
On a wooden cart, not dreaming
That his sons could make a million.

My other grandfather plumbed most of Brooklyn.
He gave up plumbing for Show
Business. All the Broadway flops
Were hauled off in his trucks—

How can I bear to dig this warehouse up?
From now on
As I dog-step through
My city, I'll
          speak
Not to men but to angels.

On our wedding day we climbed the top
Of Mount Carmel. To keep our promises
We lay down in maize.
Who can tell us how to lead our lives?
Now in Manhattan's pastures I hear
Long processions of the compact cars
Nuzzling their gasoline.
The day is springtime. Have I come too late
To hear the Zen Professor speak of peace?—
"One thing is as good as another," he says, and eats
Salad, wheat germ, and all natural foods.

Voices out of records: terrible sounds.
Wagner's music is a tongue.
My radio announces man in space. This
Was once my city. Who will tell us
How to lead our lives?

Eichmann stalls in the judicial stables.
His children saddle him to a black horse
Motoring through six million beds of grass.
He wears a light-wool suit tailored for summer.
The doctors say that we are doing well. We shall
Be cured of childhood if we keep
Counting our nightmares in the fields of sleep.
I shear black cars and records in my sleep.

Eichmann drops as man is shot in space
Out of a popgun. In our universe
A lonely husband needs a hundred wives. Who

Can tell us how to lead our lives?

The
Vaudeville
Marriage

At nineteen I married. My Lord you.
Lowering my head, I looked at the wall.
Called to, a thousand times, I never looked back.

I walk into the pharmacy of sleep.
It often happens
After I am lost
Like some rare bird
That never could be caged

I look for you
Where trees are empty,
Where leaves
Fall like prescriptions
From the trees.

Old spring umbrellas
Bloom in the looking glass
As if in preparation for thunder.
I cannot find you here,

Cannot remember.

A Greek ship
Sails on the sea
Carrying me past
The islands
Into an unknown
Island where
The burros
Are sleeping, houses
Are white, and brown
Honey is sold in
The general store. That's
Me up on the hill,
Living with the
Man I'm going
To marry. There
We are. He plays
The violin
But never practices—.
I fold and unfold
The nylon blouses
I brought from
America and put
Them neatly in
A drawer. It's
Time to go out.
We explore the island
And at the same time
Argue about
Getting married.
We walk close to
The sea, which happens
To knock our eyes
Out with its blue. An
Old lady, call her a

Witch, passes us by and
Asks us the way to
The post office.
We continue on the rocks,
Walking by the sea. "I bet
We look married," I say,
And turn my eyes from
The sea. "Only to
An old lady going
To mail
Letters at the post
Office," you reply.
And begin to weep. Not
One snorkel—
That will float
Us under the sea
To schools of fish
Who are enjoying
Their mateless
Existence—will
Take us away from
Our troubles. The
Young girl folds
Up her blouses and
Begins to pack.
The young man
Picks up his fiddle
And places it
Back into
The imitation
Alligator case.
The island
Now is sinking
Beneath the blue sea. And

The life plot thickens.
Wait.
We have forgotten
Our footsteps.
We must cover them up
To
The post office.

In the stone banks of Cliffada
Angry words
Burned like the bright melon seed.
In the stone banks of Cliffada
We drank
      Coca-Cola.

The piano played all day. He
Played a violin. I sat on a barrel,
Sun-struck by the sea, and Bach poems
Flew into me.
Village without roosters,

Flowers and crosses. There was a small boy
With a violent temper. He threw
A hive of golden notes at me.

The Snake Island.

Up on the hill we stuffed millions of secrets
In each other's throats. And swam
Without clothes. And admired
Underwater brides. Larger crustaceans
Clothed us in rainbows.
What was it we did?
That funny way of falling
Out of bed.
Hydra had no cars. Only small boats
And the island Furies
With pink tits.

The Snake Island!

Move away
From the dance deck of fact and live in
The mind
Where purpose lasts
As long as the dance lasts.

Let us begin with fire. Enter four flames
On the stage. Followed by men in white
Who lift the flames in their arms as if they were
Swans.

Do not forget water. One knows
That water is never irrational. The
Sensible water maidens arrive at the stage
Where they must contain themselves. The
Adagios of the water cooler. At last!

And the wind. It asks nothing more
Than to blow. Let the dance of the air conditioner
Make a sound
More terrifying than the sound of wind.

End all the dances of reality with a dance of
Pills. The long prescriptions of reality. Each pill
Taking the place of thought—the pill
For headaches and tranquillity.

The creation of the object,
The imagination of the ordinary,
A statement between the body
And simple used things.

The ignorance of space
Is vital. As if one were dancing out
The facts of things.

In the feathery museum—

Marriage bonds like silky ribbons snap. You're on
Your own. Over the staircase,
Over the widening stairs,

Climbing and entering.
We walk around—
I hear my high heels clicking on the floor. We
Stare at the statues—Imperial Chinese Ladies
Stuffed in glass cases smile behind white porcelain frowns—
Walking down hallways—classic vases
Robust under glass—miles away from Greece—
And bronze statues dancing—here are the Degas nudes—
You say they look like me—all twirling around
And we are walking down toward the Rembrandt room.

We stare at those eyes. At the impossible mouths
Almost about to speak and tell me some secret:
You say, "They are all close to death"—no, closer to sleep,
All of the portraits just about to snooze.
I want to lie down with you,
Discovering your limbs softly with my hands
As though you were also
A trip through an unknown museum—
In a long sleep of teeth and lips
I would kiss you so many times
As you come to life in my arms.

It was summer on Boulevard Raspail.
Our bathroom walls were peeling to light pink,
Brushes and combs were missing teeth on
The bath shelves. A box of soapflakes
Stood by the bathtub waiting to transform me.

Tacked over the sink,
Painted de Kooning wenches torn
Out of *Art News* magazine
Were staring down. They didn't like
Being placed over the sink where no one
Knew who they were.

I looked like one of them: pouting, angry, hair always messed,
Spending afternoons inside the tub
Whenever my husband took off for more than a week
On a concert tour somewhere in Lisbon or Brussels. Desperate—

I soaked in Paris. Scrubbing the loneliness
Of my skin. Frightened. I missed him
And needed the bubble baths to keep me from crying.
I sang in the daily bath. And thought sometimes of drowning.

Tub thoughts: when I was about fifteen
Some girls held a contest in boarding school to decide
The easiest way of suicide. A history major,
I quoted the Romans: "Bleeding in the bath—preferably
With slits in the arms. And loads of rose petals."
Tub thoughts: Paris—
It comes back
The bathtub filled with white detergent—Fab
Which made the bubbles in the tub as high
As an Eiffel Tower when I cried.

Now who was it

I really felt like drowning? Was it myself? My husband?
Or de Kooning?—his
Painted American women screwed up and frustrated inside his mind,
Now paper witches hanging by my tub. American
Women—locked in my bathroom—
Where they peered at my eyebrows, ears, and feet
Without the shrewdness that would make them great. O
Those young women—scrubbed and
Tubbed before they went to bed at night like children,
Washed, dressed, helped into pajamas,
Tucked into mighty dreams with creamy faces,
Saying their sexual prayers.
The painted women that I could not drown.

I became aware of needing a lover
One afternoon as I lay in the tub
And stared at my knees. As I looked at my toes
Planted near rusty fixtures,
I began thinking of a soap opera that might be called
In Defense of Love.

I then chose my lover. A modest music teacher.
I jumped out of the tub,
Rang him on the phone,
And finding him at home
Where he happened to be writing *A History of the Opera,*
I said, "All the pleasures
Of the opera are awaiting you."

He entered the bathroom elegantly,
His dyed hair smoothed by pomade, the shiny strands greased black
Over gray, his mustache
Waxed for this special occasion. To improvise: he joined me
In the tub, where I awaited him

Under the detergent.
How easy! The ecstasy—
Our electrical field of water and shock,
The short-distance field
Exposing us to
Washcloth and soap.

Somehow I want to say—to get it "across to you"—how moving
That bath was, the two of us sitting in my tub.
Those large soap bubbles in our mouths

And ice-water changes.
Our two bodies danced in a sea of detergent
And our dangerous arias.
There were no limitations to our city
When fables and swans
Splashed in the marble.

I cloaked him in a terry-cloth robe
And lifted him, gently, from the bath.
We turned and waved good-by
To the water.

De Kooning's maidens watched us back out of that bathroom
As we slipped from their extraordinary reach.

Attacking household objects with her dreams,
She takes apart
The night table, the bed, the frying pan, the cups.
She breaks in her hand
A collection of cords. Now she unfastens
Nails in leathery chairs. Tears at the horsehair
Springs under woolen beds. Blows up
Pillow feather in a puff of sleep.
She's opening up a wooden violin: no music is
Inside. Only toy green paper bills. Dollars
Were glued in music that everyone heard.
Coins were crackling under piano keys. And
Opening up the mirror, in the lead,
A collection of termites
That swarmed,
Unseen,
Chewing up the faces of our lives.
She moves. Blind termites go flying
Out of glass. Were they
Planning the destruction of our nights?
Her memories create new useful things.
Now she begins
Her strange procedure of singularities
As all objects stand
In their nude beginnings. "Wake,"
Says Manina. "I have made furniture
Out of the wicker sun with the coils of my palm."

Good-by, Old King—
Were you the straw that broke me in half?

Far away in the spice land
Where camels—five-six-seven—
Marched after Sheba on her way to Solomon,
In a place of stairways and bearded soldiers,
Clumps of tree houses, sand, and white colors,
Far away in that triangle land

You and I were not afraid
To take off our clothing, lie down to sleep,
Hug shoulder to shoulder and embrace,
Were not afraid to enter in
Battle: masculine-feminine
Where neither you nor I could win.
You dressed for breakfast. I combed my hair.
You gave me advice
And the kisses of morning—
You gave me advice extreme as
Heaven and extreme as hell. You
Gave me advice. But it all
Collapsed.

Inside the mirror
I fight, as usual, to be alone. Now in the mirror wise
King Sol
Advises me to soap my hands and face.
He stares and watches
As I brush my teeth. He asks
Me to be quiet. To lie down.
To take a cold shower. And close
My eyes. Nerves keep popping from inside my eye—
Inside the red corner. I will not die
Nor lie with you again. Although I am

Far away from that land of spice
Where the last straw doesn't break the camel's back

And little painted kings and queens
Meet in the afternoon, sit down, and talk.

My dad was a practical man.

O his big belly is gone.

Father—what's all this?
Poems to sleep on—
A gift from your daughter
To whom you remarked, "You can't
Be sensitive and sensible
At the same time." Why not?

We were angry at each other
For being sensitive and senseless. My father,
It was said,

Wore his heart on his sleeve
Because he was free
Of ambition. Like a woman
He conquered, if at all,
By surrender. When he gave in
To death

I came to life and wrote
This down. Now he lies
In Valhalla shouting,

"Daughter, why are you singing?"

It's awful how the dead can carry on.

Remember the cook who was so bad
He jumped out the window?

Everything turned out wrong.
Simply, I just didn't follow the recipe
Everyone said I should.

Cooking up a scene: I began
Without quite knowing what I was doing.

Then I was crying
And people around me asked, "What's her name?
And someone on the floor said, "Make her stop screaming,"

And someone—in a new housecoat—said,
"She should lie down," and then
The police came. It was all pretty embarrassing.

When I'm at the police station
I try to control myself. No one protects you

Unless you look calm. I protest, "Sorry, Lieutenant, I
Didn't know what I was doing,

I really didn't die,
I only pretended to." It was lovely making believe I was dead—
I looked in the mirror and said, "With so much love to live for—
Really now!"

And it ends with my cooking up something about being sad.
It is only because women are hysterical
When no one waits at home to rub them down
With conjugal castor oil or say, "The meal was good, wasn't it—
Now how is everything?"

I'm sick of New York. That's why I often go shopping.
"The life of this woman hangs off the rack of infinity."

The tram
Goes up to the top of the peak
And we are always finding ourselves
On top of the jade mountain.

Always finding—

I want to cry, "I am
I am a sea person,"
And watch the white buildings
Rise to the zodiac

Or run into the tunnel
Where the tram ends. In the tunnel
I found a scale
And stood all day on the scale
Although I was weightless.

I'm leaving my house—
Going on to another house. I'm leaving
This living room with the pink satin couch,
Pictures that balance on wire, the soft
Gold umbrella lights. I'm off
To the house of my love.

The skin of my love is soft. The hair
Of my love is soft. The lips of my love said,
"Leave the city,
Leave the jokers and glass
And smell the curl
Of very soft hair."
And the more he told me
The more I wanted to try my luck.

"I want you to know, my love,
I am from a distant land
Where everything is dead as the dead man's bone.
I would have you know
That my house and city have burned."
That's how I came
Naked to my love. He said, "Soon, you will
Find out!" And I could not tell.
But a sign said, "Take his mouth,"
And I took his mouth.

In case you have not seen me
Walking away from—

In case you did not see me
Slamming the door on—

In case you did not watch me
Say good-by to—

Birthday books, animals, trees, and shells,
The gold shields, the long cigarettes—
Let me tell you this: I'm off
To another house.

And going is easy. Easy as entering sun.
I went out of the word *sun* into the
Silent sun. Out of the
Rooms.

On the top shelves are round hatboxes
Without hats. Hats on the next shelf.
Beneath the hats are wigs. Hands and faces
On the next shelf down.

What was I called in that dress? I invented
A name that went with the sleeves. Lace
Fans that I wore when I entertained
In ridiculous get-ups. Don't go! The closet's
Not torn down. The shoes below. The shoes
On the heels much too high. Pockets, hems fall. Belts
Are hanging around
Hooks. And a small drawer
Filled with duds.

The next time
Visitors come
I shall invite them to inspect
Our closet. We shall go into my mothball pockets
Finding old letters to mail
And hilarious buttons.

Deep deep into our sleeve-selves
Where the loose stitching falls apart.

I saw the love-insect
Circling my rented room for hours,
Brushing the night table
And the piano, preening
With his passionate
Antennae.

And just as he was opening his mouth
To tell me something I had not found out,
He dropped, by mistake, in an
Ashtray and began
Fluttering in desperation. O he
Was so beautiful
And slowly made. I stared
At the love-insect
As he flapped about
In cigarettes
Until he
Got up
Out of the ashes and began
Staring back at me
In desperation,
Telling me something
I have not found out. That night

I woke up bitten by his
Life. Small mounds were
All over my body
As if my perfectly good life
Had suddenly gone bad. "Why do you love?"
He asked me. "Why do I live?
I live to scratch. And you live to bite."
I had never seen
Such an annoying and peculiar pest. "I live," I said,
And could not lie,
"I live because you cannot die."

"Get rid of your childhood your childhood your swanhood."
"It's not so easy." Getting rid of a not-wanted
Wild feathered childhood. Not so easy
Varnish and soft pillows
Getting rid of that swanday those long days
Not so easy. Getting rid of a swan.

Tell us how to begin. I was not shown
A way to speak of pain
When we were young. Embryos, fighting to be born,
Say, "Time to hatch your life." But where do we begin?
I was not shown
A way
Although I listened to the lizard's tongue
And heard the stars lamenting as they glide
Into the foaming zodiac.

And when the time came
I rode to Newark in a rented car,
Reading a book. Juggling up and down,
I was still, if you can imagine, reading
Fairy tales. I read of the Princess of China
And the Princess September. I read of the Fishbone
Princesses and of the Princess Etcetera. At the

Newark Airport
Two nurses carrying
Pocketbooks picked me up. They

Blindfolded me. Beyond my blinds
I saw houses
Of white brick, plaster, orange cement. One building
Was called "The Caprice." I
Thought of the Princess of Newark. The Swan Princesses. Varnish
And soft pillows.

When the car stopped
I entered the doctor's apartment.
The décor was Chinese. The chairs
Were Oriental. A charming trained nurse
Washed me up and down. Then, in a white room,
A doctor behind a mask—perhaps a woman,
Perhaps a man—took out my childhood.

In the midst of this operation
I lived in a castle of blood. That is
How I rid myself of the swan. Talk
About being: I look

For my swanhood, my not-wanted long day of wildhood,
Invent incubators,
And decide the time of hatching
Since I am talking

All about feathers and childhood.

Pee-wee, Tut-Tut, Jumbo-Jelly—all wild
Boys. Blond lion girl friends
Combing out their hair
Scratching with their hands. Are you afraid
Of that? Of what?

Childhood. Gangs
Turning math shelters
Into caves and Miss Fowles
Breaking through Math
Bushes with her whip
Of bright red pencils. Mad

Pavilions. Tennis
Brawls. Umbrella trees.
The empty tables
Of the dining rooms.
Cloak rooms and

The boys
Silent on the assembly porch.
So silent now. Why don't they
Holler and scratch?

I hid in the English
Shelter to recover and weep.
The books were growing
Sticky at the roots. And I hide from
Them. Pee-wee brats

Who tag me in dreams, back and forth, back and forth.

Hello.
I was a brat
Walking alone with forbidden cigarettes,
Gathering up soiled linen, basketballs, hockey sticks,
Letters from home, odd shoes and all
Things that were institutional.

I walked in a nightmare. Walked always near the woods
Escaping authority. Dreaming of being a great
Tap dancer or female comedian. Puffing and thinking,
"No! Acrobatics are best!" as I rose
In the boarding-school sky
And no one was lonelier there on the swinging
Trapeze.
Fat brat!
Escaping all the authorities.
But it wasn't a dream,
And that was the
Forbidden wood—
Hallooo. Do you see what I mean?
I ran through the deep woods wondering
If I had invented the school—or had it invented me?

When I was twelve
The trapeze snapped. The school
Began to wake up. Why

Think that destiny's more than is packed into childhood?

After you marry go riding

And you dream of a horse.
Eyes saddle him,
You go carefully next to him
Admiring his muscle formed like your own,
Cup your legs over his body,
Ride him through bed sheets and pillows,
Blankets, walls, and the moon,
Fix toes in his stirrups, legs cupped over his belly,
Your own flesh yoked to his flanks and mind,
Try riding with the ease of loving
As you gallop past deep fields of childhood
Riding past children.

Riding past childhood and death—
Nostrils open and close
As you kick with your baby heels
Over old fields of violence,
Kicking into the sides
Of the horse whose name never matters
As you ride for your life's sake.

I think of the anguish of slaves
And open my veins. Buy carnations
And drink canned nectar. It is absurd
To look for you in the
Marriage bed. You're on a Greyhound
Bus riding away.

I write to you
Thinking of the way you combed your hair
Over the sink. To you—practicing
The fiddle in the dark,
Driving down highways
In your banged-up car. Gods are the loneliest
Men. And heroes make their
Women slaves.

Ladder of love,
Hold me now.
Climbing on bare feet,
Hold me now.
Women can no longer love. Hold
On tight. I am writing
This letter without
A pencil.

It is too dark here to tell you
What I was saying—
You will soon be

South. It's dark in my city. Such
Evidence is little to build on. But
It is all I have.

How are you? Your picture's in this copy of *Life*.
All the blood
Drained from your lips, a faceless snapshot grinning
Like a tortilla, a crisp-faced pancake
In this room where I eat my heart out. Hero!

My old pal, how are you?

On the bridge we walked—mind-singing,
You were a great friend. Now, what are you doing?
Scholarly hero, all you said was right. Your
Trap dropped me into
Insight. I walked with you through all that madness
Singing, "He is not mad. He knows what he is doing."
Until our bridges started burning.

I walked through the dark. And grew
To think of you as someone who lived long ago—
A prince of memory. Friends asked me how you were.
I left the task of *being* up to you
And walked through the city singing
Until the bridges were bleeding. Tell me

To go to sleep. Dream. You can follow,
Old sweetheart, bad boy, naughty fellow,
Why don't you step from the magazine? Now think of our stage:

This cast is memory. I mean—at night—
I think of our fantasy. All the rest
Is paper.

My shipping king hated the sea.
He owned it. He knew it.
The boats were all his mistresses
Going crisscross over the sea,
Then returning home.

That's why he left his worry beads—
Those black beads that turned human in his hands.
He wanted to travel inland. O

Atlas moved the guests out of the palace. His garden
Was copied from the Arabian Nights. Women
Changed into eagles. Men into bats. Waiters were sulky
Sultans carrying beef. Maids were bored slave girls. Statuettes, pink
And sprouting water, turned into the Seven Atlas Daughters.
Chauffeurs were waiting parakeets. Cooks—golden parrots.
Dumb acts and animal acts. Single women. The
Odds and ends all
Part of the vaudeville.
Abracadabra. The
Illusionists carried several gold umbrellas.
Escape artists, ventriloquists, all
Part of the spectacle. And
What was Atlas dreaming
In his garden while cognac
Was served by the floodlit pool? "I've
Got the world by the balls," he thought. Then,
Atlas looked down in his pool and cried,
"I can't see my own mouth move in the water."

Of course it seemed
Impossible to live
This loony kind of
Life. Neither a
Daughter nor anybody's wife.
It could not be understood. I
Wanted, often, to give it all up. But
Couldn't think
Of how
To live my life better.

Afraid to come near
Me. All my old friends. It is,
I think, a lot due to
The flames. I'll eat some grapes
And then go out. Walk
In the sunspots
Of my lady life.
Sometimes it's good
To keep out of the house.

Rented a horse today
From Montclair stable.
Took reins in thumbs
And posted in the park. I wanted
The horse to gallop
But he wanted to trot.
A swift kick
Is what he needs.
Under the horse's
Belly I looked for his reins.
Got distracted
By all the earth's brown leaves.
Even when I fall off
I can't keep my mind on

What I'm doing. And I am
Always falling. Always falling.

To toughen up
I went fencing. Put
An iron grill
Over my face.
Under the mask
I was learning
Only how to defend
My face.
To forget
I went drinking.
Jean was my
Companion. He made
Me start crying.
Friends are
Better than steeds: watch
How swiftly
They run away.

Heartbreak's not
Good for you. Examined
My heart. Reached in deep
And pulled it out. Saw
How the heart continues
To beat hours after
It is removed from the body. Put
My heart back
In my head by mistake.
Listened to my brain—
That's my heart
Burning inside with its tick
Tock tick tock tick
Tock.

Walking around. On Third
Avenue—unmarried
Saints dressed in blue
Velvet
Seem to be heavenly
Policewomen. I arrive
Late as usual
For our appointment. And feel
Shabby in my sweater.

Know that life is odd,
Not even. Even
Sex is oddly even.
Where is that Garden
Of Even? All is odd.
Nothing even.

Four ducks on a pond. The
Sky beyond and
White clouds on
Wings. What a funny
Thing to remember
For years. To
Remember with tears.

Dreams of a woman:
I wanted to have a child.
Name her Alice or Anne.
Only this
Remains in my head.
Decided to
Put it down.

They say I'm loose
In the head. My heart

Goes ticking
In the cup of my eye. Always
The body's a mess.

I dress and undress.
Want to remember
The horse
That rode me through the park
And the odd
Sensation of getting even.

The likeness of all
Things: Instead of the sword
A heart. Instead of
The angel a dog. Instead of
The head a walk
That went into flames. Then
My room and everything in it. Now
Tear this up. And
Go to battle.

All is, of course, odd,
Not even. Flames
In the mouth. A furnace
For heaven. When grapes
Are gone, flames
Are eaten.
"Speak from the fire,"
Someone said. So
I did.

Each dial leads to a voyage of its own.
On the white wall
It has a shape of its own—now it's an ear.
Secret cords lead to it and from it:
White bones that spiral to impossible
Tongues. And a voice saying,
"Do not be afraid."

Afraid of what?
Phony plastic bone,
Drops of sound dumb as tympanum,
White ear doldrum down
In luxurious whispers of secret
Adulteries,
Long-distance confessions
Of friendship and mystery voices
Announcing the time or again
And again "Do not be

Afraid." How else will she
Comfort me—her voice curling
Alphabets? And to whom
Do I press my lips
Zipping haystack kisses
And telling of my latest poem?

Wait a minute. They are
Beating a woman. Do not be afraid,
I wish to inform her
Through my telephone.
Hello? Cannibal? Goddess? I am home,
Minister, Prophet, Murderer, Madam,
Your loss of sensitivity's in

My stimulated ear.
And before we say farewell
Let me remind you that
You leave me
All these white waves.

For Dudley Fitts

I spoke to the Marriage Dancers, whispered to them
To crawl out of the crumbling hotels
While the earthquake shook
The island of Manhattan with a gong
That might have been
The Bell Telephone ring.

What was I saying to the Marriage
Dancers? I was saying, "Get out quick"—that is to say,
Get the hell out of this island that is itself
A sort of hell. Get out of the telephone directory,
For God's sake,
Get out of the Manhattan Yellow Pages—out of maps,
Get out of Convent, Lexington, Pleasant,
Get out of Boiler Repairing, Washington Machine & Welding
        Works,
And Tom Wizard's Auto Repairs,
Get out of Chemicals, out of the Kramer X-Ray Co.,
Jump out of Heat,
Jump from Precision Heat to Insect Killing Devices,
Get out of Lightning and Limousines and Wheel Chair Travelers
And the Pioneer Business Record Center,
Marriage Dancers jump from Complete Packaging Service into
The Wolfahrt Studios Incorporated, my God,
Get out of the Seafare Restaurant.

Dance out of Installations, out of the Card Dialers,
Princess Phone Wall Telephone Home Speakerphone Telephone
In color—can you hear me? And

The Marriage Dancers leapt out of the Yellow Pages
That were yellow flames, walking fingers, then walking feet, then
Dancing feet—arabesque—over the flames of
The city.

I had one more call to make and that
Was to the people on my island
Who were unhappily married
And would remain so
During the earthquake. I had to tell them
And rang them up secretly
And asked them why they moved out of each other's beds
And into each other's beds
Without hearing each other walk,
Without hearing each other speak, either
To themselves or to the other. It was
As if they were all standing
On separate balconies.

I wanted to tell these couples to stop leaving each
Other before they reached each other—
To stop pulling each other's eyelashes while tears came down. Stop
Ripping each other's tonsils when lips met,
Stop pulling at each other's sexes. The radio played
And the television and the Victrola now
Hi-fi played from several speakers. But there were no speakers.
They never spoke to each other and
That was the trouble I wanted to tell them
Before the flames began—before the earth
Opened up—they should speak and dance
With each other since they might still be dancing
Beneath the earth in sickness never in health.

But I misplaced my own voice
Somewhere in my house.
I have looked under the telephone,
Beneath two pink sofas, both stiff as lips,
Inside hatboxes, underneath my chair. And
I have searched beneath the table

And beside the lamp,
Looked through one linen closet and
The medicine cabinet,
Looked in dictionaries and in the sink
Wondering where my voice
Is hidden—to warn
The Dancers.

Lovers
Praise the stones, the gleaming white
Nude stones. Our
Life begins here.
In the garden
Of nothing—the stones
Stand here forever
In place of the streaming
Leaves, and the pebbles
Are raked in
Waves. Someone has joined
Secrets.
We are nude in this
Garden, nude as stones. Tonight
The moon yokes
With the summer gods but
For lovers there is
Nowhere to go nowhere to hide.
What are we saying? "Never
Mind that
Our new life is slower than life,
Never mind our thoughts and secrets—"
As old clothes,
Our clothes,
Rot in the deep grass
Folded neatly and hidden. O
There is nowhere to go
Nowhere to hide.

When idiots ask me, "How do you write your poems?"
I'll tell them, "Pink shells. Pink shells." You
Will know what I mean. Think

Of the afternoon
When the gulls wheeled over the garbage of Three Mile Harbor
And the car, my gray Valiant, was suddenly curved
Into sand. Think of us all getting out, watching it sag
Into the sand. It was only a mimic accident
But it kept us from going where we were going. As
The farm boy who came by to help ran home for his rope
I felt helpless and impatient
Because accidents are always a long waste
Of time. And I felt wrong

Leaving you staring at the car—the helpless car
Sinking like a compact gray steel whale—
But there was nothing I could do so I walked away
Down the road to look at the sea flay the rocks gently. And I think

I went to pray,
Not for the car, certainly, but to give praise
For our afternoon which had been warm, perfect as a gift.
It was then—as the farm boys were yanking the car
Out of the sand—
That I saw the shells, the amazing twisting shells,
Spirals pink, rose, calcified sea bones,
Shells in splayed conches, strange, beaten apart
By waves so that their hearts, that part that curves
And forms a peeling shelter of its own,
Were proud hosannas carved from the breathing water
And tossed to me by the wind.
I worked fast. There was not much time
Before the car was towed out of the sand. And I picked
Them quickly. I didn't want to waste a second

And gathered as many shells as my arms could hold.
I brought them back to the scene of the accident
Feeling ridiculous.
I'd been busy with sea shells instead of observing the car,
But calamities and minor accidents
Give us time to discover what is around us.

We got back in the car. As we drove by the wall of the sea
Remember that I told you that ridiculous stops
Are always turned to advantage—in improbable times
We discover whatever mystery we can. So whenever they
Want answers about the invisible
I'll tell them, "Pink shells. The pink shells," and

Think of the accident, Alexandra,
Think of the pink shells!

The Never-Never man swims in my mind
And entertains me. We were once
In an aquarium.

We'd swim around in that exotic pool.
I'd keep him company. Then I'd go home.
He swam to me over the telephone. Asked
Me to come back into the pool. At that time
I was young. A butterball.
That's all clear as crystal. What I don't understand
Is why Never-Never dangles in my mind.
Zip up the lid. Wonder about the book.
Picture him now: Poor lost
Fish. It's the mind
That keeps me indifferent. I cannot explain.
The Never-Never man was at least his own ghost.
Swim back to me.
Sealed behind glass, he
Whispers, "Never-Never."

Having burned all our islands
There was only one left. And we went
There—on the ferry—avoiding
Various friends connected with old disasters.
When we arrived, the island
Was empty. We were carrying our belongings
In plastic bags, and talked
Of a seaside house
That would never belong to us. Looked
For a place to stay. A sea place
With a bed, where we could lie down
And joke. Love each other. Smoke. Sink
In that bed, performing the Wreck
Of the Hesperus
On a bed that didn't belong to us.
But there was not one bed.
Not one house. And remember this?
We found white sea dollars
Under the very white sand.
And we slept in the sand.

The fireflies scared us to dig
Deep and make our hole for sleeping in.
I remember your sleep
As I sang to you. We were cold and you
Were breathing as if in pain
Since we had run
To the island of Mull, knowing no one,
Only our own names. In the morning
That strange silent wind came. I woke up
And saw a fisherman—was it a joke?—
Holding a bleeding gull in his hand.
And in my dream
I was that gull in your hand.

It is all on another hill.
The ferry ride. The lost island of Mull.
That beach without a house. And the man
Who was also you—
Holding me high to the wind.

The Enemy

For Ce Roser

This summer
I'm at war with everything.
I'm jumping to knife the eggplant in the soil.
In the garden every vegetable
Grows as swiftly as it can. Tell me why
I am so impatient!

A woman's life is
Waiting for a stranger. Waiting
Takes too long! Sometimes
I think I'm locked up on this farm
Like some wild prisoner waiting for her King. On
Rainy afternoons I read *The Supreme*

Doctrine—"Keep alive," it tells me. And I draw a map

Where the warm
Foam slaps on the sea. Deep-sea
Fishing last week. This week I visited a home
For helpless animals. And found a dog.
His friends came visiting. And my new log,
Half novel, half helpless diary,
Records my life. I'm happy
With what's done. But writing out my childhood
Takes too long. Impatient
For the fall. I want to see the leaves
Turning away for good. I want to see
The landscape when it's all
The color of the sun. I'll watch the garden bleed heigh-ho

And sing: I looked for the enemy
Who was my King.

PATTER

Nothing is less innocent than two people
With a sense of humor. Take this young lady and
The comedian. She's intellectual. Romantic. He's almost untutored
In the finer arts: reading and writing. A realist,
He looks for his name in *Variety* and *Show Business,*
Keeps on a diet. Will not leave his wife and kiddies.
She lives alone. Suddenly gets thin. He's reading
Rimbaud. She studies vaudeville. She's making him read,
Taking him to museums. She's losing weight
And reading *Variety.* She thinks of placing
An ad in *Variety:* Young Girl Falls Flat For
Comedian. He's a looker. She's not
Show Biz. She's now wearing false lashes and
Hairpieces. Something is goofy. A show for
The Palace. He's reading
And she's writing hunks for comedians. O long
Copacabanas. How can you tell me that these people
Aren't freaks? They are not people at all.
He says he is trying to make her "more real."
She can't break through his cakewalk. She's figured
Out he was a comedian in the Garden
Of Eden. He says she has a personality that would
Revolutionize the Ice Business. She's so friendly.
He has no emotion. She has too much. He's a realist.
She's a dreamer. He wants fame and fortune. She
Wants to lead a good life. He makes her get skinny. She
Makes him lose his mind. And his zest for sleeping. Reading
All those poems. They do a man-woman act. It never
Goes over. Then they try the School Act. The Storyteller
And the Dramatic Sketch. The Stump Speech. He's
A ventriloquist. He keeps telling her what to say
And think. "Even if I wasn't married I wouldn't get married!"
Why not? "People like us shouldn't get married." Why not?

"We're not people." What are we? We are the acrobatic act
With complete somersaults.
Magicians. Wire acts . . . I tell ya
It's real hard work in Hollywood if one
Takes the profession seriously. You know all comedians
Are really tragic. I'm very strange. Silent. A freak. I don't
Belong anywhere. And have no desire to be Show Biz. I have no
    friends.
I'm shy. Unmaterialistic. Did you ever get those guys?
I'll go back to my life with an appreciative feeling
For having met you in person. Your act was educational
As well as entertaining. I'll look for your name and you
Look for mine. I think we should see less of each other. I'll call
Ya tomorrow. I'll really never
Make it. I'm not Show Biz.

SUMMER

Ho ho for my yellow summer. But are they really funny,
The paid comedians who mock
Their desperate lives to get applause? I know
My joker is lost
Inside movie reflections of despair—
He's working in Hollywood this summer. And playing
Golf. His secret is:
He knows that he's grotesque.

Solitude's best. I spend my summer on a rented farm
Not far from a run-down golf course. Yellow's here,
Lopped in the sun. And the grass
Is better than any wit. I see the grass
Bending in wild hilarity
To be so green. Summer is nearly gone.

Mornings I ride a yellow horse
Over the yellow field. When I arrive
At sunflowers we halt. I must slow down
And watch round yellow turning in the wind.
There's something in the long and awkward stalks
Of sunflowers that is hilarious.

Summer blends its wit with my sea-farm. Funny
Sounds: Bird calls and horses swatting at the flies.
I talk to clover. Is that what is funny?

"Help me to be alive," I say to the sun.
The sun turns its deep spotlight on my sport:
"It's your own life you're riding!"

LAS VEGAS

My night-club comedian
Can no longer be found
In the Garden of Eden
Making a call
Across the country to his girl,
Can no longer be seen
In the sauna baths
Where he sat,
A great man
Sweating out his dreams.
He has left his golf course
And deserted his voice teacher,
He's forgotten his elocution lessons
And singing teacher.

His lips
Turn upside down,

His pompadour is gray.
All of his combs
Fall down.
My conceited Happy-go-lucky
Can no longer be found in the Eden Garden
Where he was the great tree and the snake,
And joker, make no mistake, he was Adam and Eve too.

He's on the telephone—Hello? Las Vegas?
Upside-down world,
Glittery old horseshoe world,
Open-door fun palace
Promising stargazing and learning machines,
Gag world open twenty-four hours a day
For mad conversations,
Dream center, mad booth of lemon kings
And roulette-mongers,
Place of winnings and losses,
Wonderland of cactus and roses,
Golden Nugget Singing Eden.

I hear him
Braying in his flat voice:
                    I gotta go now.

IN MY SLEEP

The child tells his story.
The ladybug is his friend.
The spirit is his enemy.
The caterpillar eats the moth.
The careers of Barnum and Bailey and the Ringlings
Are depressing the children's government.
The top! The top! He knew it

Would spin forever. Animal acts: He
Could tame a flea. Whip
The clown. Frighten the lion
Out of his crib. The life of a cowboy—
Who is that in the saddle?

WINTER

The laughter of the comedian
Is a turning point
And the last thing in my mind.

I can't stand
Up to the patter
Of the lonely comedian.

In Manhattan
Snow was forecast by
The radio. But never
Appeared.

The snow will see me out. But
After that—?

More than the snow is falling.
The world's doing pratfalls
And for all I know
Blessings
And bruises are all mixed

Up. I'm breaking up

With the stand-up comedian—
A comedy I seem to confuse

With the end of the world.

"I'm not falling apart,"
I say into the telephone
To the voices that talk back to me,

"But tumbling into a sea
Where I keep my head just
Above water."

Love
Letters
from Asia

I have made love to the yellow lilies,
Turned my face against their cool skin,
Led my lips and eyes to their stamens
While I cried to see anything as bright
As these golden lilies.
How I look for them!

There are people who do not explore the in-
Side of flowers, kissing them,
Resting their own tongues on their petals.
I must tell them. Where will I begin?

And I love
Earth, violently, and vegetables,
Stars, and all things that will not break.
My hair smells of melons, marl, jasmine.

What I wanted
Was to be myself again
On a Monday morning, to
Wake and wash with cold water
And soap, to dress
Swiftly and walk without
Thinking
Where I came from, who I was,
To be silent and
Saved
From the long days of myself.
It no longer mattered
If I burned, bursting,
Then catching fire. It
Was enough to have
Known the war within
Myself and to be tired—
To be sick of the
Boundaries—to have
Lived in the calendar of the
Brain where one meets
One's self each day in a talking
Mirror and says, "How long
Are you here for? When
Will the war be over?" I wanted
A sea change, a place
Where things grew into
Secrets of color,
A place I imagined of festivals,
Rocks, brilliant
Reptiles, trees
And serious things—wind bells
That chime—a place
Where I could be useful.
We moved, quite suddenly,

To the Colony.
I saw ancient women
In their tennis suits
Playing all afternoon. Their men
Played Business, Journalist,
General—others were
Involved in Domestic Monopoly—
And some played
Sailor on the sea. I lived
In their fashion,
Going in and out of the
Moments. If it were not
For the fish
And melons,
For the queer atonal
Music and water slipping
In the cracks of houses,
Olive fresh-water snakes,
The strangeness—
I might have
Become a part of the Colony,
Seeing myself in that life
In which all things
Are at the height of themselves.
I might have eaten mangoes,
Had my picture taken,
Written postcards to friends
Announcing my recreation, gone
On gaping at bar girls
And bargains, and having
Coats made by
Overnight tailors.
But I must tell you this:
One morning I woke up
And entered life;

I ran quite swiftly through the mountains,
Passing the palm trees and civets,
Watching harvests
And children
All in the ripeness of summer. It
Was then
I inherited joy
The way one inherits a fortune.

This ancient Chinese man with white-,
Blue-, and red-striped socks, white
Shorts, hat, white hair, old skin,
Moves quickly on the court,
Looks across the net, and says,
"Each time you move your racquet
It is
The closing of a door. Lifting
The racquet, moving it across
Your chest, across your heart—
The closing of a door.
The closing of a door."

I move across the grass,
Awkward, unathletic,
Thinking of the past.

As the swift game continues
I drive strokes past
Camps and boarding schools,
Japan, three years in France,
All the voices
In the flame trees saying,
Love me. Use me. Use me
To see everything, as
One by one
My ghosts sweat and work out
Beside me,
Swinging
Their helpless arms
Into the sky.

The
White bird
Circles over me
Wearing a crown. He
Must have escaped
From a country where
Chinaberries dangled
From the green trees
Against yellow
Skies, where ebony spleenworts
And branches
Were dazzled by the wind
And where
His great crown
Was made. O bird! I exhale
And inhale your secrets—my
Heart beats now like
Yours
As I lead you home alive.
I am quiet
As I move through
The twigs as if they were
Clouds—I am what
I always was—a child
Leading
Birds out of the sun.
The weeds are quiet now. I
Listen to imaginary
Woods and grasses—gullies,
Trees, ponds—
None are as real
As your white pearl feathers
As we fly

Through the parables of
Trees while I call to you, "Bird! Bird!"
Crying again
To be so young.

We wake. Our day
Starts on the Peak: we are
Singing and burning
Our secrets. All night
We turned in the same sheets
And now we share the day.
We dress, lace our shoes, run
To find the end
Of each long walk. There is none.
Up on this high wild hill
The dangling birds
Open black fringed umbrellas
And bob
Invisible through fog—blackbird
Umbrellas,
Shielding gods.
How free,
How easy, our life
Here. There's not
Much to do
But read or answer
The doorbell. Our
Long talks,
Like water blending into
Water, have
No end—and no
Start.
Old loneliness
Goes flying with
Birds down
The green hill.
I have achieved a life that is natural.

Women peel
Thousand-year-old eggs
By scraping off mud
From the colored shells. Under
Great fish heads bleeding
On a string, we
Are discovered walking
Hand in hand
In this market where
Everything's possible.
We have arrived
In this human place
Of sea-horse medicine
Where sugared kumquats
Shine in glass jars
And spiders and rats
Parade through vegetables. Here,
In this winding street,
A lazy boy
Holds Chinese oranges
Inside his hands
And spends all morning
With a rubber stamp stamping
Them "Sunkist" so
They'll sell for more. Here we
Touch elephant horn—black
Tusks and ivory—
Here we touch thin private scrolls
And rims of porcelain,
See wizards carve flowers
In white mah-jongg cubes. My
Senses open wide
And make me dizzy. Water bugs
That will refuse to drown
Burn on our sandals. Vendors

Show their teeth
Of golden stones. Suddenly, ducks,
Pressed with sleepy eyes,
Hang over us like rows
Of tennis racquets. Snakes
Are pulled out of
Baskets to be eaten. And the sun
Presses against us. Starting
From where we are,
Let's go down, down, down under cabbage and
Ginger, let us escape
These ducks and taste our lives. Under
The blood of animals
Let's turn our own lives inside out,
Throwing away petals
We cannot hold—
Families, deaths, marriages—
Discarding our histories,
Those exits and entrances
We cannot explain, mistakes,
Odd people, countries
We have slept with,
Throw ourselves
Down under dragonflies, broccoli,
Under the pythons, crushed medicines,
Spices,
While our silly tongues scratch,
Our new bodies touch,
And we are always ready to be born.

NIGHT SWIMMING

I remember that slow island
Where you took me, once, in Asia
Where the crabs had great shields of thick light
And carried, on their backs, worlds of their own.
We copied them.
The phosphorescent water tucked us in
That ocean where we will not be again
And phosphorescent water held us down
Like two stars spinning, binaries that bobbed
Into the mangrove waves. Green
Diamonds cut our lips and we became
Constellations, partners near the moon.
Seaweed lit our nipples as we swam
Through silvery schools of fish. I
Did the dead man's float and then I called,
"Hurry. We must return!"

THE BEGINNING

With my fingers
I design blue mosques and temples
On the linen, trace them
On the pillows
While my child
Puffs like a pillow in my flesh
And changes to a moonstone
Or a pearl. Tonight
My marrow flowers into coral.

And shall I dream, again, of minarets?
I live inside these temples

While the child
Grows in the great bulb of my shaking belly.
I see myself dance in the mirror's shards
Where life is ocean-heavy. Life begins—
Oh, dance with me until the ocean ends!
Once time and blood cells bobbed like barnacles
Scratching at my heels, until
I left those cords and bones. Now
Nothing's known.
Child,
Will you float my marrow to the world
And tell them who I am? Now you
Curve gently like a baroque pearl. And
As you swim through the yolk sac will you glide
Into this world of linen and new life?

THE EYES

Today your face
Grows rapidly.
Eyelid and
Ear shine
Under my skin
Like melons. We, roped
Together,
Float
In the universe
And one root
At a time, one
Vein at a time, we
Shift and I sleep
As your new eyes
Begin.

THE HANDS

White sprouts
Are opening. Are they
The new, soft hearts
Of peonies? ginger lilies?
Under my stone sea-snail
Belly, under that place
Of snow and sunlight,
Ivory anemones
Blow up inside me
And mushroom in the billows
Of my flesh. I ask myself
About the grace of fingers.
Fingernails,
Like bleeding hearts,
Grow under stones. I wake
And listen to what they
Have to tell me: "We are dumb
White flowers
Under the foreign side
Of the moon."

LOVE SONG TO THE UNBORN

Where the spinal cord gets hooked up to the past,
Where ancient loves
Get married, drowned, or lost,
I hook with the starfish.
Our joy is without spine. I rake
The faces out like clams
And wake, turning in pain.

Late summertime. My back

Is well again. How strange
Now to be able to lift things
Or open windows. I must unbend
And throw off blankets,
Unfold by the sea.

Now, by the beach, my toes
Are white roots inside water.
When it rains
I wait for the sun,
Snoozing inside the damp sheets
On this farm
When it is warm.

I lie on my back, flat on a pumpkin field,
My flesh puffed like a gourd,
The marigolds twined around my thighs.

Find me in the deep splash
Of pumpkins, squash,
And green leaves that prickle.
I rub my fingers on the skin
Of squash—skin white as papyrus,
Smoother than porcelain—
And look up at the sun.
I know that its strength will be your own.

Here tangled yellow flowers
Pinch like fingers.
You will be here next summer,
Singing of pumpkins in your ripe spine time.
Love, I take down this landscape in my mind.

I shall meet you at
The instant of your birth
When you emerge from the red leaves,
Dripping from the sea shells in my skin.

You have been swimming, too,
Against the salt weeds
Under the red leaves.

Then I shall meet you,
See you, and tell you how many mornings
Of my life

I have been sleeping
Under the flame trees,
My veins splayed

Like the veins of leaves
Reaching beyond me
And caught in the air.

For I have always
Wanted to be born, to be
Reborn each morning,

And in your beginning
I find my own meaning.

What shall I say, what
Shall I tell you
When I meet you
For the first time?

We shall meet
Face to face
In the great, burning

New-leaf beginning,
Your first
Red leaf
Moment, then,
Of life.

Love
Opened my eyes to the amulets
Of trees—
Green leaves, falling miracles,
Falling, one by one,
On the street. In Japan we bought

White porcelain tipped into palm-eyes
And icicles, pots shaped like
Peach stones and glazed in sky blue.
We touched the rims of the world's glaze
But arrived without anything. Then

You gave me my own room without old things,
Without decorations, without paintings
That hang on the walls
Only to become new walls themselves, without
Shapes that interfere
With what I must be.

My dreams were unshaped and unpainted, I
Lived with the fantasy of the sea—shaped
Always on the verge of words. You—
Looked for emptiness the way lovers seek sleep,
Burned currencies
And seeds of your own beginnings. How easy
For us to change into firebirds, fly
Past history, oceans, striking against the sky
With our own new wings. Now—

Shall we return where we came from?
You be the brush that strikes.
And, burning inside, still burning, I'll
Live as the flaming kiln that shapes the pot.

At home for a week I have been spying on fruit.
In the immense bowl the fruit has ripened
And begins to change. The colors darken at
Their edges and turn black. New shapes
Explode and warp—adding new odors
To our rooms. Sap falls out of their skins,
And, at a certain point, they change
Their shape entirely, becoming both
Substance and sap. They are so
Magically changed
When they have been in a room too long. I watch
These shapes changing from green to a darker
Green—yellow into black, orange into
Black, as if all bright colors must go, finally,
Into darkness, burst, or turn to seed.
I wonder if
All trees
Are offering only a pure excuse for words—as if
Language itself were falling
From the trees, apples
No more than the boundaries of words. Ripeness. Language.
Metamorphosis. This is what I am spying on, sitting
Patiently with silent flies,
Watching these forms of life turn mad and giddy.
Mangoes, custard apples turn, unbend,
And all become something else.
If only there were a perfect word
I could give to you—a word like some artichoke
That could sit on the table, dry, and become itself.

It is Monday morning
And the goldfish wife
Comes out with her laundry
To shout her message.
There! Her basket glistens
In the sun and shines—
A wicker O. And see how
The goldfish wife touches
The clothes, her fingers
Stretching toward starch,
The wind beating her hair
As though all hair
Were laundry. Come,
Dear fishwife, golden
In your gills, come tell
Us of your life and be
Specific. Come into our lives—
Where no sun shines and no
Winds spill
The laundry from the rope—
Come on the broomstick of a
Widow-witch, fly
From the empty clotheslines
Of the poor
And teach us how to air
Our lives again.

All beaches are the same.
This was the landscape
Of my girlhood. I belonged
To great arrivals at hotels,
My uncle's girls,
The women's tennis matches,
Snarls in the nurse's wool
As she knitted me sweaters.

Why unwind the dead?
Say I was one
Who looked for the world
Beneath the blue
Sand bucket, who searched
All day for China
In the sand. I
Waited for
Blue magic ships,
Billowing sails,
To come point-blank,
God, and discover me.

Open me. Close me,
Shout the dangerous women
Sitting around the pool doing nothing.
Open me up, they are saying, their
Lips great pocketbooks
With shiny clasps. Inside the lobby
Ancient tourists sit
Dressed in nylon, talking
Lip to lip.

Under the secret flaps
Of beach cabanas
Ideograms pour over the
Women. Old numbers, letters
Fall on their hair and nails
As light lives in the pool.

How amazed I was, when I was a child,
To see your life on the sand.
To see you living in your jelly shape,
Round and slippery and dangerous.
You seemed to have fallen
Not from the rim of the sea,
But from the galaxies.
Stranger, you delighted me. Weird object of
The stinging world.

That was China! Where blue
Tiles spanned half the world—blue
Feathers hammered
By the sun. Poets wise
As Solomon
Whispering in the gardens,
Walking between gold pebbles,
Quiet, joyful, practical men.
Not one of them could be labeled mad.
All in another lifetime,
Great marble lions chiseled
And refined by water. I envy
Those poets—not their king. He
Was another thing—as we can
Imagine—seeing the broken
Columns of his city and
His clothes,
Now strands of dust sealed
Inside museums. They said,
In those days, "Poets
Are our kings—we'll bury
Them in tombs larger
Than homes!"

I envy their affection,
Brilliant as colors,
Their lightheaded kindness
To each other. They took
Long walks and held each
Other, fingers clasped in the open gardens.
In their gardens
They exchanged new songs
And secrets.
Time was on their side

As they placed silk caps
Upon their black and glittering hair
And walked out, proudly, in
Their sun.

Living new lives
Above sea level, we have forgotten
Undersea landscapes.
Tidal zones fall like towers
At the ocean's rim.
The sea divides itself into three realms:
The Zone of the Shallow Seas, the Zone of Light,
And, beneath that, the end of the sea—
That secret and silent Zone of Perpetual Darkness. These
Zones are no longer our concern.
Slowly we came to this gentle place,
Walking past stones, trees,
Dry earth, shacks, layers of garbage,
And were stared at
By hill people. They dared us to take
Root in the earth, dared us to break
Like new flowers without stalks. They saw us
Ascending.

Once water was necessary. We farmed the sea,
Hauling out food
From salinity. Mud, fish
Gave us our lonely lives. Waves and the tides—
Starfish, scallops,
Crabs, mussels, sea pork,
Rockweeds, and shells sharp as razors—
Gave us our living.
Now we no longer dream of sea palms,
Our memories have burned out sharks,
The feeding frenzy of killers.
We have ascended through sea weather
To the top of this mountain. Here grass
Blows in green waves,
Light falls on our mouths like rain, and
Nets of white clouds tighten around our lives. We

Are free of the extremity of the sea! Free
To live with our calm self-nature. Now—
Farewell to bleeding whales,
Oil-bearing targets for whalers' harpoons.
Our net is tightened. If we leave now,
It is not for the sea—but for the endless path
That will raise us even higher
Above sea level.

OUTSIDE

Walking around. The temple,
Quiet as a hospital.

I wanted to make a shuffling
Sound with my feet. I wanted to find

My shoulders. I wanted to look
At my toes—more than that,

Get strangers to walk with me.

I wanted to make clicking noises
Into the faces of unknown stockings and shoes,

And I wanted
To make short circles with my feet.

INSIDE

The stupas are curling as mad
As ice cream,
And the long, golden Buddha
Is candy king
In this temple.

In this temple of candy
The long, sleeping Buddha reclines. He's
Thinking of nothing. He's longer
Than any god. His toes

Take up the entire
Lower temple.

Always the dreamer is lost
As if he must be, to please us,
A blown-up balloon. Now

The shrimp priests
Bow to the giant's toe

And compare their own
Size to his. Why did they build the temple
Around the king?
They should have let him sleep in
The street near the trees.

On Victoria Peak
Prickly plants
Take precedence
Over tulips and roses,
And this is why
I prefer them
To flowers.
In knots of thorns,
The outward
Petals change into
Spinal forms,
Where blood
Turns back
At the flower
Edge.
Here everything beautiful
Can be dried and saved:
Pine cones, artichokes, thistles
All go on with their own
Silent and
Often uninteresting
Adornments,
But they seem to
Be hinting,
"Watch me. I will
Not fade."

He appeared
Without a shadow,
Crying *joy* in a language that
We had forgotten or never knew
As syllables dropped like kumquats
From his tongue and he smiled at boys
In the street who made fun of him. He
Did not seem "Western"—he was too mad for
That, jangled and put together in a shabby way
That might have embarrassed us. And from
What place in the East he had arrived we could
Not tell—he seemed to have shed his origin
The way flowers shed petals
Until only the stem remains. And he was
That stem. Thin, made of sunlight, his face burned
By wind (all the streets he had been to!),
And he wandered
Past gaps, white buildings,
Glassy windows bursting with
Jewelry, past flowers,
Mirrors—
And what he sang was again this word *joy,*
Sounding so much like a bird
Calling to his invisible mate
As he flies beyond the New Territories,
Then dips into a mountain.

Love Singer! Perhaps he once played at being
A bard in China before
Singing
In our parking lots, gardens, traffic, new
Hotel lobbies. And we listened.
And I keep asking,
"What is his name?" and
"What does he sing?" and

"What do you call that stringed
Instrument, which seems to be cared for and polished
By feathers?" Here
In this city,
Every day we have seen this miracle-monger
Walking the streets. But only once
Did I hear him speak to me clearly.

The backstage of this airport
Was unfamiliar. We sat
In the cubicle of the chief customs official
On broken wicker stools, staring
At framed portraits of great
Asian smugglers and close-ups
Of bizarre smuggling techniques.
I saw huge photos of men's shoes: the
Toes had pockets filled with opium. I saw
Suitcases with false tops.
Stowaway techniques are amazing; the pictures
Were so odd they made us smile.
Meanwhile, the potential prisoner
Never arrived. We drove back
To familiar things in this strange city,
To spend the night
Exchanging new information
Leading to the capture
Of our secret selves. Why should we
Hide our own lies
In the toes of our shoes?
Later, we knew
We had arrived,
Without knowing why
At that moment of revelation
When we threw out
The puffs and padding of
Our inner lies. Love,
After all, descends in the foreign dark,
Apparently praying to be caught.

1

Crows, pheasants, cuckoos, toucans
Crawl out of everything
With faces I once loved
In my wilderness.
In this new day turning
I arrive
Where guava and fish
Hang in the sun like flies.
In this green waking
A crab
Crawls over my eyes. Now, whatever I am,
I will always be,
And if it is death to love
I shall love a thousand times over,
Being born a thousand times
In this new day, in this new day turning,
When falcons and dogs return
To their homes in the golden grass burning,
And hawfinch and jellyfish
No longer whistle or sting.
I walk out of dreaming
Brushing off old loves like leaves—
Forgetting where I have been
For my new life's sake.

2

Mammals fall out of the sky—
Musk shrews and porcupines
Shadow us as we sigh
To be alive in this time
When we know
What it means not to mean anything.

You, for example, are
The dragonfly,
And I, in the dark, sleep
With you each night
In this gray cocoon
Located on a mountain. Here
It is timeless. Here
It is cool. We
Never hesitate
To be silent. Or say
What we both already know: each day
Transparent lilies
Trumpet our life. Mountains
Breathe, offering burning leaves and trees.
All reptiles celebrate:
Skinks and terrapins
With bright blue tails,
Green snakes and cobras,
Corals and kraits, white
And golden, climb into our mornings,
When we run out of reason
And follow, like insects
In our innocence, watermarks
Of each **miracle.**

3

This morning we picked
Birds of paradise whose wings
Were stalks,
Limbs and bones
Of mad flowers.
In the sun.
This morning we could rise

To pick the wild
Planned birds of paradise.

Sea.
The palms
Shine in the night
So they now seem
To be burning
A line in the
Sky. Don't forget
The moon
Or telling
Time by the
Sea. Am I
Bent on a life change?

In one night
And one morning
That seemed like forty
Days and forty nights,
The raindrops came—louder
And louder—breaking
Mountains, roofs, and
Bridges, knocking glass
Buildings into their
Foundations, winding
All birds and plants
Together, mashing
Squatters' homes
Into chicken bones,
Cracking the floating
Sampans in a splintered
Sea.

Sun-Tong, handsome "Ladies' Tailor,"
Known by some to be a lady-killer,
Travels no more on his motorbike
With his plastic sacks stuffed with
Pajamas, alterations, spindles;
Sun-Tong lies under the spools of
Rock, beneath great slabs of shale,
Drowned in a splash
Of dresses. "Sun-Tong, where were
You going in the storm?"

Everything's wrong. Phones
And wires broken. The Peak roads are gone.
There's no food except
For the tin cans hauled
Up the mountains by the bravest mules.
No school either. All the land

Is sliding. On this hill,
Children slosh near the gray hospital
To watch a helicopter drop supplies. It's still
Raining.

"We shall do what we like in the rain!" think
The children, innocent of death,
As they dance into kingdom come in
Their new galoshes, splashing
Near landslides, slipping away
From their houses, dancing
Behind the backs of buildings
While rocks fall down the mountains
And the world flows. Storms
Open the dark rooms
Of Heaven—
Everything drops out
Of clouds in buckets,
Bells ring, time
Stops, and
The Wind Gates chime.

Shadows
Forget
Who I
Am.
I have bathed
For the second time
Today and I feel
New. Terry-cloth
Bathrobes
Bloom
In hooked
Corners, curling
Fans and brushes
Sleep in the living room,
Flowers
Burn
Holes in the air
With nude
Colors. And rain
Strikes like
Pebbles
All day,
Forming wide circles
On the window.
All morning
I have been
Thinking
Of the organization
Of paradise—the
Wide circles of planets
Forming curls
In the sky, the
Rings, stars, and heavens
Ending

In the eye of a rose.
I see myself
Tremble in
A glass of water. I
No longer know
Who I am—or who
I will be—and no
Longer care. I am changed
By thoughts
Of this morning
And changed by the
Strong
Calm of my life. Green
Whiskered birds
Fly under my
Fingers—all urgent
Messengers
Telling what I
Know. Now kingfishers
Fly through
Trees seeing
Me through the windows,
Their wings
Tough as fish scales,
Their beaks
Tougher than yellow fruit. This
Is not all. How
Can this be all
And be so true? I
Breathe my whole life
In one morning. My room
Is balanced on a cloud,
Houses below. Mad white
Pagodas tilted in brick. Long

Walks that end in
Palms. I tremble
All day
In a glass
Of water.